LOVERS' MEETING

CATHERINE LODGE

Quills & Quartos
PUBLISHING

Edited by Ellen Pickels and Jan Ashton

Cover by Carpe Librum Book Design

On the cover: Serrure Auguste *The Meeting*, 1872

ISBN 978-1-951033-62-0 (ebook) and 978-1-951033-63-7 (paperback)

To Mum – just because

TABLE OF CONTENTS

CHAPTER 1

FIRST IMPRESSIONS

IT WAS A WARM DAY IN EARLY AUTUMN, AND MISS ELIZABETH Bennet was in flight from her home. The allure of the woods around her father's house was more than enough to tempt her away from her mother's continuing transports on the leasing of the neighbouring property, Netherfield. She did not think she could support another afternoon listening to the way her mother converted her own wishes into certainties and then shared these certainties with their neighbours in a manner lacking both sense and propriety.

As she tramped happily through the fallen leaves, revelling in the first dry day after a week of incessant rain, she wondered what her mother would do if this Mr Bingley were unprincipled or riddled with some dreadful disease. She had barely determined that a mistress would probably not be an obstacle in her mother's mind—although leprosy just might be —when her thoughts were interrupted by sudden, dreadful noises from the road, which lay about twenty yards away from her through the trees.

She had been half-conscious of the sodden plodding of draft horses and the creaking of a large cart, but that familiar rural sound was suddenly replaced with a loud, creaking, tearing noise, a crash, and then the sounds of terrified horses.

Without a second thought, she ran through the trees towards the road to find a scene of terrible destruction. A great wagon, full of gravel, had broken either a wheel or the front axle. The cart had slumped onto one front corner, throwing the entire load forward, breaking boards, and burying the driver to the waist in stones. The horses were trapped in their harness, and the sounds they made and their desperate rearing and plunging were both affecting and dreadful.

For half a minute, she stood appalled, but rallying herself quickly, she turned to run for help. Before she could do so, a magnificent carriage and four appeared perhaps fifty yards away and approaching at speed. With relief, she ran down the road and hailed the coachman.

The coach halted rapidly and a gentleman leapt from it, almost before it had stopped, and briefly surveyed the scene. As one of his footmen came to the head of the magnificent matched bays, the gentleman and his coachman ran forward and, in a few minutes, succeeded in first calming and then unharnessing the cart horses and turning them into a nearby field. Looking to Elizabeth, the gentleman removed his hat and, obviously recognising Elizabeth as a gentlewoman, bowed and said, "We shall need more men, madam. Where is the nearest place to summon them?"

Elizabeth pointed over the fields. "My father's house and the home farm are over there, the building with the red roof. A little over a mile cross-country, perhaps two by road."

The gentleman turned his head and called over his shoulder, "Young Tom, take one of the leaders and ride to the house over there. We need as many men as possible with spades." Behind him, Elizabeth saw one of the two footmen and the coachman begin to unharness one of the bays as the other footman approached with two shovels of the type normally used when a coach became bogged down.

"I beg your pardon, Miss...?" He was shrugging out of his greatcoat as they spoke, his words hurried but perfectly composed.

"Bennet." In the circumstances, it seemed ridiculous to stand on ceremony.

"Miss Bennet. Fitzwilliam Darcy, at your service." He looked at her closely. "You are obviously not unduly alarmed. Might I ask you to see to the carter's lad while Hopkins and I see what we can do for the driver?" He pointed behind her, and she turned to see a boy of perhaps ten years lying unconscious, one arm at an odd angle. As she hurried towards him, she saw a bay being ridden across the fields.

She knelt beside the poor boy, careless of the mud that immediately struck through her dress. His pulse was strong, but he was obviously going to be in considerable pain when he awoke, and lying in the wet and filth of the road was not going to do him any good. She turned towards the cart to see Mr Darcy and his footman trying to dig the gravel away from the carter, but such was the position of the cart and its load that, the more they shovelled away, the more slid down from the back of the cart, and he was forced to call a halt and direct his man to start digging out the load from the back.

"Mr Darcy?" He was on his knees too, attempting to assess the extent of the carter's injuries, but he turned at her call. "I shall need something to protect the boy from the mud."

He nodded and called out, "Tom Coachman, break out one of the seats." He turned back to her. "You had better wrap him in my greatcoat until we can get a surgeon. There was a town about two miles back—is there one there?" She assured him there was and then assured him of her willingness to ride into Meryton to fetch Mr Mason. She was a little taken aback when she realised that she would have to ride on the box next to the coachman in order to direct him but, refusing to be missish, she allowed the gentleman to help her to her lofty seat and, once they had used the nearby field to turn the equipage around, found that she rather enjoyed the ride even if she did feel a trifle unsafe. She was also well aware that her mother would be outraged at her conduct—driving through the village on the box of a strange coach—and although she was convinced that her father would support her actions, she knew he would probably do little to protect her from her mother's reproaches.

She was, however, rather relieved to make the return journey inside the coach with Mr Mason on the box. The inside was quite the most luxurious she had ever seen, even with one of the seats missing. In a net beside her, she could see a number of books and, by craning her neck, could make out some of the titles: Boswell's *Life of Johnson*, two volumes of Gibbon's *Decline and Fall*, and Wordsworth's *Lyrical Ballads*. She had read all but the last and dearly wished for an opportunity to take a peek; however, such was the speed of their journey, she could not be sure she would not damage the obviously costly volume.

When they arrived at the scene of the accident, she found that her father had arrived with his man Jesse, their butler, Mr Hill, and some of the men from the farm. They had managed to shift most of the load off the cart, but at some stage, the gravel had shifted forward, and Mr Darcy and the returned 'Young Tom' were holding it back with the aid of a board broken from the wagon. As she alighted from the coach, she could hear his deep voice talking to the carter.

"Look at me, Matt Walker, look at me," he was saying. "You were telling me about your young woman." She heard the hoarse voice of the trapped man and realised that Mr Darcy was talking to him to keep him conscious.

She hurried towards the boy, followed by Mr Mason. The lad was now lying on the missing coach seat, its fine leather ruined by the mud. The greatcoat still covered him. He was conscious and, though he must have been in great pain, he said nothing as the surgeon looked him over and then splinted his broken arm. When he was complimented on his bravery,

4

he grinned in tired triumph and opened his uninjured hand to reveal a gold coin. "Master give me an 'ole guinea not to cry out, and I didn't neither."

They covered him up, and Elizabeth stayed with him as the surgeon went over to the driver, who seemed to be on the brink of being freed. She helped the boy tuck the coin in an inner pocket and knelt beside him. Then, taking her cue from Mr Darcy, she talked to him, trying to distract him from his pain until he could be moved.

Over his head, she watched as enough of the gravel was removed that they could attempt to lift the wagon off its driver. Levers were placed and with a good deal of effort—and rather more bad language than Mr Bennet liked to hear in the presence of his daughter—the carter was dragged free. There was a flurry of activity and her father's men closed round the carter as the surgeon worked on him for several minutes before declaring that there was little more he could do in the middle of the road and that at least one leg was so badly crushed it would have to come off. Above the injured man's protests, she could hear Mr Darcy assuring him that he would be looked after and that he could count on a job on his estate, no matter how badly he was hurt. As they carried him off to one of her father's farm carts, she could hear the carter shouting, "You promise, master? You promise me?" and the steady reply, "I promise, Walker, a proper job on a proper wage, and I shall come and dance at your wedding."

The boy, too, was lifted onto the cart, complete with the carriage seat, and Mr Darcy reclaimed his greatcoat, only to grimace at its state and re-cover the boy. He offered Elizabeth his hand, and she got to her feet as her father came over. They had obviously introduced themselves because her father invited him to come over to Longbourn to clean up and take some refreshment.

"I think not, if you will excuse me. I am on my way to stay with my friend Bingley at Netherfield, and was expected some hours ago. I feel I ought to be on my way as soon as possible. If I may, I shall call tomorrow to see about Walker and young

Peter. I have assured Mr Mason that I shall be responsible for his fees, and we can arrange for their future care then." They shook hands, and he turned to Elizabeth. "May I also thank you for your invaluable assistance, Miss Bennet?" She held out her hand and he bowed over it. "It is a refreshing change indeed to meet such an intrepid young lady."

She looked at him sharply, alert for signs of mockery, for she had just begun to realise how far she had trespassed beyond the bounds of everyday propriety. He appeared to be all sincerity, so she curtseyed and stood by her father as the wagon was heaved out of the way, and the coach, now reunited with its full complement of horses, was manoeuvred past it and up the road towards Netherfield.

CHAPTER 2

WHAT THE NEIGHBOURS SAID

THE WHOLE OF THAT PART OF HERTFORDSHIRE WAS AGREED: it was quite the most exciting thing to have happened for many a long year, eclipsing entirely the housemaid who stole Mrs Goulding's silver teaspoons and even the occasion Hoggart's bull escaped on market day.

It was greatly regretted, however, that the nearest observers were Lizzy Bennet and her father. The former could not be trusted to tell the tale without turning the whole of her own part into a jest, and the latter could not be induced to tell it at all. In desperation, Meryton and its surrounding district were forced to turn to Mrs Mason, the surgeon's wife, who, while not exactly a lady, was really quite genteel and could certainly be entertained for tea at Mrs Philips's house if not, perhaps, at Longbourn or Lucas Lodge.

"Yes," said that lady to a circle of eager listeners. "He quite insisted on paying for everything, including a nurse to sit with poor Walker and then for a further operation."

Young Robert Lucas interrupted at this point and demanded, "Was there lots of blood?" He was promptly sent home for not behaving like a gentleman in the presence of ladies.

"Mr Darcy is not exactly a jovial gentleman but perfectly polite, didn't quibble about the expense. Do you know he went to see Hoggart and paid for the damage to the winter wheat in the field? Because of the damage by the horses." This, everyone agreed, was particularly generous, especially in view of the size of Hoggart's family, which was so large as to be scarcely decent.

"I did ask how long he would be staying." The circle leaned forward eagerly. "But he said he was at the disposal of his friend and could hardly say." The circle leaned back. "His card says, 'Fitzwilliam Darcy, Pemberley, Derbyshire and Darcy House, Grosvenor Square, London.' A very genteel address, I believe." This was much more gratifying: a house bearing his name, and in Grosvenor Square, no less. Speculation ran rife as to his marital status and income, the latter of which rose with every speaker until at last it was decided that he could not be worth a penny less than five thousand a year and very possibly more.

Mrs Bennet, as usual a charter member of her sister Philips's coterie, was in ecstasies. A quiet, generous and, above all, rich young man. Did he not sound just the man for her Jane? For, of course, the ladies were all agreed: he must be single. So long as he had not acquired a disgust for the entire family from the regrettably hoydenish ways of her younger sister Elizabeth. What on earth had she been thinking? Riding around on the box of a coach like that ancient British person Mr Bennet kept calling her—Bow-legged Caesar or something of that nature. She had no compassion for her mother's nerves or her family's credit.

The ladies with daughters of their own to dispose of sighed and were obliged to admit, to themselves at least, that if the polite Mr Darcy were to take to any lady in the neighbourhood, Jane Bennet, the acknowledged local beauty, had by far the greatest chance of attracting his attention.

At home, Mrs Bennet laid siege to her husband, demanding that he call on their new neighbours immediately. "A rich, young gentleman arrives in the neighbourhood and might very well escape entirely if you will not help me to contrive a meeting with our dear Jane."

"Escape, Mrs Bennet? You make the poor man sound like your lawful prey. Perhaps he has no desire to marry. Perhaps he might prefer my Lizzy. He was quite taken with her intrepidity."

"Well, she ought to have kept it better covered. No, I am quite resolved. Jane will catch his eye, for how could she not? And since I have it on excellent authority that his tongue does not run on wheels like some people's I could name, he will do very well for her. Perhaps this Mr Bingley will do for Lizzy if she can learn to behave like a lady instead of a hobbledehoy."

Mr Bennet, who had lingered over his dinner much longer than was his wont, rose to return to his library. "Well, as I have no doubt you will see the whole party at the assembly, we can judge for ourselves which way the gentlemens' inclinations lie —always assuming they are allowed any."

If Elizabeth had been exasperated by her mother's suppositions when she had no information, the volume of such, once a very little information was available, were such as to drive her to her father's library for sanctuary. However, even the normally phlegmatic Mr Bennet could not resist twitting her on the loss of so fine a beau to her sister, and since the weather had closed in again, she was left to attempt to retain her temper and good spirits without the aid of the vigorous exercise on which she had come to rely.

CHAPTER 3

DAWN THOUGHTS OF A MAN OF PROPERTY

FITZWILLIAM DARCY AWOKE JUST BEFORE DAWN AND LAY IN BED, waiting for his man, Lawson, and wondering, not for the first time, how a man as exhausted as he could possibly sleep so badly.

He watched the light growing in a small gap between the curtains of his chamber and, from force of habit, compiled a list of his duties for the day. Time to show Bingley how to ride an estate, what to look for, and what not to notice. There was no point in objecting to what the locals had taken while the place was empty as long as they now realised that such tolerance was at an end. Then they should check out the willows down by the river; they looked ripe for coppicing, providing that was allowed under the lease.

Then he had to write to Empson about the Chambers' business and to the Overseer of the Poor in Lambton. (He was by no means satisfied about the administration of outdoor relief, nor did he like what he was hearing about the proposed new Poor Law.) Then he should ride over to Walker's mother's house to see how he was doing, which, with any luck, would absolve him from calling on any of Bingley's neighbours with him. (They looked like a bucolic lot at best.)

Lawson came in and busied himself setting out the shaving tackle and his master's riding clothes. Sometimes Darcy felt that the only time he was truly alive was during his morning gallop—even around the prim and manicured hedgerows of Hertfordshire. He was eight and twenty, for heaven's sake; when had he started to feel like a man twice his age? Every morning, he awoke to a growing heaviness of spirit, a settled melancholy that reminded him only too well of the last years of his late father. Every day, he tried to rouse himself, to shake himself free, and despite the riding, scrupulous attention to business, and his every effort, each night he lay awake, waiting for a few hours of sleep and the dawn that always came too early.

It was, he knew, rank ingratitude if not blasphemy. He was young, he had his health and his faculties—not like poor Meopham, dying of the French disease in some forgotten corner of his father's estate in Cheshire where no one need ever see him. He shook his head angrily. No, he was counting his blessings: youth, strength, more fortune than any two or three of his acquaintance put together. He had no right feeling like this! He flung the blankets aside and made ready to face the day.

He sat as Lawson shaved him and realised he had not written to Georgiana since Sunday. He hoped to hell he had done the right thing in sending her to stay with his cousin Viscount Summerbridge and his wife. Summerbridge was a bit of an ass, but Lady Eleanor was a decent, kind woman and, after a difficult confinement, had just given birth to a daughter to join their two sons. Georgiana was fond of the little boys, and she would be company for Eleanor. He had promised Bingley months ago to come and help him with his new duties, and he was not going to leave Georgiana alone all day with Caroline Bingley and that horse-faced sister of hers. Not the least disconcerting thing about his current state of mind was the knowledge that his usual equable temper had deserted him, leaving him prey to sudden rages he had to fight hard to contain. One day Miss Bingley would go too far, and he would lose Bingley's friendship forever by telling her he would as soon marry a fishwife. His father would have hated that. *"A gentleman does not show anger, Fitzwilliam. I am seriously displeased."*

Had he been alone, he would have shaken his head. Another thing his father would have hated. *"A gentleman never grimaces, Fitzwilliam. His thoughts are his own."*

His clothes felt big on him; he must have lost more weight. Another thing he must remember to take care of. If *he* noticed, so would Georgiana and she was quite distressed enough. He had tried and failed miserably to persuade her that she had not lowered herself in his eyes and that his current distraction did not have its cause in her behaviour. For the first time in their lives, his assurances had not carried the weight of law to her, and he did not know what to do. Thank heavens, Fitzwilliam was due back from Portugal at Christmas; perhaps he might have some idea of what to do. At least he could talk about it with his cousin without being told that it was time he married.

It was not that he did not intend to do so at some stage. It was just that Pemberley was so isolated, and he always felt so damn hunted in society. Poor Meopham, whose family's pockets had been to let for years, had once drawn a caricature of him as a cornered fox surrounded by a pack of baying mamas and daughters with teeth like bears, while a bevy of beautiful women waved hopelessly in the background. Presumably, there must be intelligent, well-read, handsome, unmarried women out there somewhere; why did he always seem to meet the stupid, the ignorant, and the insipid? He supposed it was hardly their fault that they were so badly educated, but did they have to be so damn incurious? Like the one who told him her father could not be a Whig because he wore his own hair!

He took his hat and gloves from Lawson and remembered to thank him. *"A gentleman is never unappreciative, Fitzwilliam. Servants like to have their efforts noticed."*

It was a cold day but bright and windless. He shrugged into his greatcoat and went outside where his horse stood skittishly, eager to be off. He rode away from the house across the fields breathing in the scents of autumn, and ignoring as usual the urge to ride and keep on riding until everyone and everything he knew was left behind like so much dust.

If only he were not so damn tired.

CHAPTER 4

THE ASSEMBLY

ELIZABETH WAS NOT FORMED FOR MELANCHOLY OR THE practice of dwelling on the many disadvantages of her family life. There was an assembly planned in Meryton, and she dearly loved to dance, so she cast aside her irritation and joined her sisters in the business of making the best of dresses, slippers, and ribbons. Their aunt Gardiner had sent them recent copies of magazines with the latest modes, and once she and Jane had persuaded Lydia out of a headdress suitable only for a woman twice her age and Kitty out of dampening her muslin to make it cling, they had all settled on new arrangements of their hair they felt were both attractive and fashionable.

Mr Bennet had, as usual, declared his fixed intention of avoiding the occasion, and even Mrs Bennet knew there was no moving him from his library. So the Longbourn coach was crammed with a squirming cargo of ladies, each attempting to protect her own gown from the feet and elbows of the other passengers.

"And remember, Jane: Mr Darcy is the tall, dark gentleman, and you must be certain to look your best when we are introduced. And as for you, Miss Lizzy, I will thank you not to put yourself forward. We do not wish to give the gentleman a disgust of our country manners."

Elizabeth hid a smile and wondered what her mother would say if she told her that she had met the enigmatic Mr Darcy again at Mrs Walker's house when she had called to ascertain how her son was faring. The gentleman had been perfectly polite, but there had been a distinctly disdainful expression on his—admittedly handsome—face. No doubt he disapproved of her visiting Mrs Walker because the woman ran a small alehouse, although she had taken her father's manservant Jesse as escort. Perhaps he shared her mother's views on 'country manners'.

The assembly rooms were full of light, music, and their friends. Lydia and Kitty immediately ran off to join a group of younger girls while Mary found a quiet, well-lit corner in which to read. Jane was commanded to sit with her mother, and Elizabeth escaped to see her friend Charlotte Lucas, who was sitting with her mother on the other side of the room. The band, while not the most polished Elizabeth had ever heard, were enthusiastic, and the overall effect was good-humoured; even those not dancing could scarcely avoid tapping their feet.

Elizabeth was soon invited to dance by Stephen Goulding, a friend since childhood, and she enjoyed an invigorating cotillion that lifted her not very depressed spirits and lent a becoming flush to her cheeks.

However, the set was just drawing to an end when the party from Netherfield arrived with all the éclat of a royal visit. Not only was the hero of the hour present but also the new proprietor of Netherfield, a good-humoured-looking blond man of perhaps five or six and twenty, and two further ladies and another gentleman, quickly identified as the latter's two sisters and a brother-in-law. Their very dress marked them out amid the less fashionable crowd they had joined. The ladies' silks had been costed to within sixpence before they had advanced ten paces, and the gentlemen's' incomes had been confidently stated on the basis only of the weight of their broadcloth and the probable cost of their silk neckcloths. The latter were tied in knots of such intricacy that at least half a dozen, hitherto entirely satisfied, young gentlemen were cast into deepest gloom.

Sir William Lucas, as the acknowledged leader of Meryton society, hurried forward to greet them, and bows and curtseys were exchanged. He also took it upon himself to express the thanks of the neighbourhood for Mr Darcy's actions following the accident.

"I beg you not to refer to it, sir," replied Mr Darcy. "I did no more than anyone might who came across such an incident." This was felt to be most gentlemanly. However, once he had danced with both ladies of his own party, he refused to dance with anyone else. This was felt to be most ungentlemanly, but since the entire town had but recently decided that he was everything that was good, they were all reluctant to change their minds so quickly and determined that he had probably injured himself somewhat during his recent exertions and was unable to continue.

Mr Bingley, while the rest of his party held themselves aloof, was apparently determined to make up for their refusals. He danced every set, was profuse in his compliments in a manner that happily combined good sense and propriety, and was evidently much taken with Jane, whom he asked to dance twice. Mrs Bennet did her best to attract the notice of his friend, doing everything possible short of tripping him, and that gentleman eventually took refuge on the other side of the hall where he surveyed the company from his considerable height in a manner that either revealed his disdain for his company or his physical discomfort, depending on whether one believed the jealous Stephen Goulding or his neighbours. Since the former considered himself a Radical and his neighbours considered him to be the next best thing to a French Revolutionary, his opinion was completely discounted.

Mr Darcy had taken a position quite close to where Elizabeth was sitting with Charlotte, and the former might well have been the only person to hear an exchange between two of the newly arrived gentlemen.

"Come, Darcy," said Mr Bingley, "I must have you dance. I hate to see you standing about by yourself in this stupid manner. You had much better dance."

"I certainly shall not. You know how I detest it unless I am particularly acquainted with my partner."

"Upon my word, I would not be as fastidious as you for a kingdom. I have never met such a group of pleasant people in all my life."

"You might recollect, Bingley, that one of these 'pleasant people' owns the cottage I visited yesterday. I would not keep my pigs in such conditions."

Bingley laughed and shook his head. "If you are going to assess your dance partners by their fathers' concern for the poor, I am afraid you may end up with a dance card entirely full of Quakers and such. Well, I have the hand of that remarkably pretty Bennet girl for the next set, so I shall leave you here in lofty contemplation of your own virtue."

Mr Darcy watched his friend collect his partner from her harridan of a mother and wondered how much longer they would have to stay at this affair. It was his own fault; he had encouraged Bingley to attend, knowing how important it was for him to get to know his new neighbours, but he had underestimated just how uncomfortable he himself would be.

He winced imperceptibly as the band struck up once more and, as he did so, caught the eye of the Miss Bennet he had met twice over the last few days. *No*, he thought, *Miss Elizabeth. Bingley is dancing with Miss Bennet.* He sighed to himself; he could hardly ignore the girl, so he bowed and braced himself for another exchange of polite nothings.

They traded greetings, then: "You are not enjoying the music, Mr Darcy." It was much more a statement than a question.

"I am afraid not, Miss Elizabeth." Really, he did not need to explain but found himself adding, "Are you familiar with the expression 'perfect pitch'?" She nodded, and he continued. "The second violin and the viola are both tuned flat, and I find the noise something akin to that of fingernails on a slate with which my cousins tormented me when we were all learning to write."

"You are a musician, sir?"

"I played the violin at one time," he replied stiffly. The conversation was becoming much too personal for his comfort.

"Oh, what a shame you no longer do so. Music is such a resource in times of both trouble and joy."

He bowed but said nothing, and they watched the rest of the set in silence.

It was the last set of the evening, and the assembly soon broke up in a flurry of lost shawls, mislaid sons and daughters, and a welter of promises to call. Lydia and Kitty had had partners all evening and were satisfied. Mary had found a kindred soul in a visiting cousin of the King family and had spent all evening discussing the works of the Reverend Fordyce. Jane had danced twice with the highly sought-after Mr Bingley, and if she had not managed to attract the attention of the rich Mr Darcy, he had not danced with anyone else from the town, so Mrs Bennet was almost satisfied.

Almost, but not quite. "Lizzy, I thought I told you not to thrust yourself forward in that immodest way. You quite kept Mr Darcy from meeting Jane."

Elizabeth shook her head. "Oh, Mama! You can hardly blame me for his hiding himself away all evening. He hardly exchanged more than a dozen words with anyone not of his party and certainly not with me." Her mother did not hear, but this was nothing new; Elizabeth was resigned to her mother not hearing anything she did not wish to hear. They returned home with no more than the usual amount of gossiping and complaining.

In the Netherfield coach, the conversation was much less good-humoured. While Hurst and Bingley dozed, the latter's sisters were united in abusing the company, the music, and the hall. They both, and especially Caroline, tried to recruit Mr Darcy to their cause but without success. That gentleman cradled his hat on his knee and tried to remember when he had stopped playing and why.

CHAPTER 5

ANOTHER CHANCE ENCOUNTER

Occasionally on her daily rambles, Elizabeth saw at a distance the two gentlemen from Netherfield surveying the estate on horseback and was glad that Mr Bingley bade fair to become a conscientious landlord for the period of his tenancy. The flooding down by the willows, which had been known to affect her father's land, was being addressed, and workmen were set to improving the hedges and ditches.

Opinion in Meryton was further conciliated by many of the necessary purchases being made there and not, as had been feared, in London. When the two men arrived at church on Sunday, what little doubt remained was finally removed.

Elizabeth, sitting in the family pew with her parents and sisters, had an excellent view of Mr Bingley and Mr Darcy and noticed that the former was often adrift in his prayer book and that the latter would patiently find the right page for him. Moreover, and to her delight, when the clerk gave the note for the psalm, Mr Darcy listened to the usual uncertain murmur, led by her Aunt Philips's penetrating but uncertain soprano, before joining in with a beautiful, confident baritone which the congregation thankfully accepted as a more promising lead; the rest of the service was much more melodious than it had been for a very long time. She also noticed that, unlike many in the church, he seemed to have some serious subject for prayer, for he remained on his knees for some time, head bent and brow furrowed.

After the service, the congregation stopped for the usual exchange of pleasantries, her father particularly wishing to invite Mr Bingley to discuss the land drainage problems common to the two estates. After several fruitless attempts to interrupt and secure the gentlemen for dinner, or tea or, indeed, anything, Mrs Bennet swept off attended by all her daughters except Elizabeth, who was talking to Charlotte Lucas. When the latter left with her parents, Elizabeth elected to wait for her father and thus found herself in company with Mr Darcy.

They exchanged stilted civilities, exclaimed over the unseasonable warmth, expressed their hopes for continuing dry weather, and quickly ran out of civil commonplaces. She glanced over at her father, still expounding, apparently oblivious to Mr Bingley's growing bewilderment. Elizabeth knew all about her father's ability to appear oblivious.

However, she had no idea just how very pretty she looked, her chestnut curls clustering beneath a most becoming bonnet, the delicate flush of her cheek complemented by the dark burgundy of her ribbons and spencer. She raised her face and smiled gaily. "I really must thank you for your assistance with our singing," she said. "I have seldom heard us make a more 'joyful noise unto the Lord'. Are you all as tuneful in Derbyshire?"

He looked uncomfortable but replied. "I hardly know. We have a parish band in my church at home. Do you not have one here?"

"Alas, no. Ever since our serpent-player argued with our only violinist, we have been left to our own meagre resources, and I am afraid we have just demonstrated just how meagre, meagre can be."

He did not reply, and for some reason she preferred not to examine too closely, she felt she had to fill the ensuing silence. He had not replaced his hat when he had left the church, and she nodded towards it. "As a small child, I always wondered why gentlemen seem to spend the whole service gazing intently into their hats. I was quite disappointed when I found out they did not hide interesting books in there." She smiled ruefully. "I am afraid I was not a very pious child."

"I have a cousin who was particularly and ostentatiously pious as a child. I'm afraid it always induced in me a desire to kick his shins during the sermon." Now, what in heaven's name had induced him to say that? He recoiled, physically stepping backwards, mentally attempting to regain his usual composure. He was arrested by a low gurgle of laughter.

"Then I am delighted to have met a fellow sinner, Mr Darcy." Her father hailed her at this point, and they parted with the usual civilities.

As he climbed into the coach, he reproached himself harshly. This was another complication he could well do without. If he were not careful, he would find that he had created expectations where none could be met.

"I say, Darcy, you had all the luck there! You got to speak to a handsome young lady, and I got cornered by her father to talk about French drains and rights of turbary, whatever they are."

"You would do well to listen to him. Local knowledge of drainage is highly valuable: the heavy clay down by the river will be extremely difficult to deal with."

Bingley merely grinned, tipped his hat over his eyes, and prepared for a short nap before Sunday luncheon.

It was, perhaps, unfortunate for Mr Darcy's peace of mind that the company at Netherfield was particularly tiresome that day. Hurst slept, and his wife and Miss Bingley's criticisms of the neighbourhood, the amusements available, and the gentility of its inhabitants were unusually harsh. He could have ignored all this had Miss Bingley's attentions to himself not been more than usually blatant and annoying. Why on earth would she think that choosing the second volume of the book he was attempting to read would recommend her to him? Next time, he swore to himself savagely, he would bring nothing but Plato in the original Greek and see what she did then!

He was conscious that his temper was only thinly held and, after dinner, escaped to the billiard room with Bingley, who was a wretched player but at least was not interested in marrying him.

The next day, Elizabeth was walking the woods between Netherfield and Longbourn when she met Mr Darcy leading his horse. It was the quite the most beautiful animal she had ever seen: glossy, black, and powerful. Its erstwhile rider hailed her with relief. "Ah, Miss Bennet, you come most happily upon your cue once again. Tell me, am I nearer Netherfield or the local blacksmith? My horse has cast a shoe."

She dropped him a curtsey, a little lopsidedly because of the muddy lane. "I believe you had better return to Netherfield, sir. The nearest blacksmith is in Meryton." He looked as though he would have cursed had he been alone; instead, he passed a tired hand over his face and thanked her for the information.

"You have a truly splendid horse, Mr Darcy." She fumbled in her pocket and produced an apple. "This was intended for my own breakfast, but I would far rather devote it to this beautiful animal. Pray tell me, what is he called?"

He watched narrowly as she held out her hand with the apple balanced on the palm, although whether this was in consideration for her fingers or for the horse, she could not tell. She laughed happily as the apple was plucked gently from her.

"His name is Suleiman."

"Ah, The Magnificent! No wonder he looked so condescending when he took my poor breakfast."

To her utter astonishment, a smile broke over the usually stern face above her, and a very becoming smile it was too. Suddenly, he looked much younger, and she realised what she had forgotten since the accident: that he could not have reached thirty years of age. "Believe it or not, Miss Bennet, you are the first person who has ever recognised his namesake." Then, apparently thinking he had made a blunder of some description, he seemed to recollect himself, bowed, and took his leave in as few words as were consistent with the barest of civility.

She watched him go, reflecting that he was quite the most puzzling person she had ever met.

He strode away, cursing his body's betrayal. A little wit, a pair of big brown eyes, and there he was—strangled in his small clothes. Thank heaven for long coats.

But she had looked so… Standing in that muddy lane, her cheeks flushed, little wisps of hair clinging to her forehead beneath that cheaply made bonnet, an apple in her hand, an Eve to his Adam.

He slapped his crop against his leg. What was happening to him? This was not what he was, and he could not even blame her! She was friendly, witty, charming, and had remarkably beautiful eyes, but he could be nothing to her, and she obviously expected nothing—at least not at the moment. But how long would it be before her appalling mother noticed his attention and started throwing the girl at him? It was bad enough when she tried to interest him a girl to whom he had never spoken. *A gentleman never raises expectations that cannot be met, Fitzwilliam.*"

He trudged onwards, his riding boots slipping in the mud, and suddenly, it struck him forcibly that she was probably lonely. He had never met anyone like her. What chance was there that there was anyone else like her in this godforsaken backwater? He imagined her in a house with that mother and those three younger sisters; he might not have talked to anyone at the assembly, but there was nothing wrong with his hearing. The eldest had better manners and seemed to be no fool, but there was no liveliness there, no spark. But as for the other three: the middle one had not the sense to hold her tongue if she had nothing to say but sententious platitudes. And the two youngest! One was a pale, insipid imitation of Miss Bennet and the other a bloated, vulgar version of Miss Elizabeth—loud where she was vivacious and ill-mannered where she was playful. He had seen Longbourn from the road, and there scarcely seemed room for the whole family and a father who, according to local report, hardly ever left his library. At least at Pemberley there was peace and room to hide.

He had to avoid her. It was only fair to her.

It was nearly dark when he returned to Netherfield and handed Suleiman over to the care of his groom. Darcy was cold and wet, and it took a real effort to climb the stairs to his chamber to change for dinner. Lawson, a prince among valets, had secured hot water, and he bathed thankfully, feeling sensation flooding back into his hands and feet. He bowed his shoulders for the jugs of warm water and knew he had no grounds for complaint. He had a life not one man in a hundred thousand could boast, and he had vowed on his knees he would remember that.

As he came out of his room, he met Bingley in the corridor. "There you are, Darcy. Caroline was worried you had come to harm."

"I am sorry if I worried Miss Bingley. Suleiman cast a shoe."

Bingley put a hand on his arm. "Look here," he began awkwardly. "I do not want to pry, but…well…I can see you are troubled. If there were anything I could do—you would tell me, wouldn't you?"

To his horror, he felt his eyes sting. "I must apologise if I have seemed inattentive or—"

"No, no, that is not what I meant. It is just…you know where I am if you need my assistance."

The intention was undeniably kind, but the effect was the opposite of what was intended. He now felt all the burden of having imposed his unhappiness upon his friend. He had to conquer this—he had to. Tomorrow he would work harder, try harder—exhaust himself body and mind so that he could sleep. And perhaps, if he were not so tired, he might be able to work out how to bring himself back under good regulation.

In pursuance of his vow, he spent the following day with Bingley, walking the property and trying to share with him the years of experience his father and Pemberley's stewards had instilled in him. *"You belong to the land, just as much as the land belongs to you, Fitzwilliam. You owe it your best."*

The estate was only leased, but it was never too early to begin to learn your duty.

However, when they were driven back to the house by driving rain, they found that Caroline and Louisa had invited Miss Jane Bennet for tea, and by the obvious contrivance of her mother, the girl was now stranded and suffering from a heavy cold.

What followed next had an inevitability to which he could only surrender. Elizabeth Bennet arrived—vital, unafraid, and most winning of all, genuinely concerned about her sister. She was in the house; there was no escape without rudeness so gross as to be completely beyond him. He could only listen and watch.

Everything about her seemed admirable.

One evening, returning to his room to dress for dinner, he heard her in her sister's room, talking to one of the maids. "Have you heard whether your sister has had her baby yet, Sukey?"

"Oh yes, miss," was the reply. "I saw our Davy after church on Sunday. Fine little boy, pair of lungs on him like a bull calf."

"Oh, I am glad! After poor little Matilda, that must be a comfort to her. My sister and I shall be calling to see her as soon as we get home. If you have any message you would like to send, we would be happy to take it." He tried to imagine Caroline Bingley visiting tenants and smiled wryly.

God help him, he even admired her music. Yes, she ought to practise more—she confessed it herself—but there was a sincerity to her music, a sense that she played because she had something to say and not merely because it was expected of her. He caught himself wondering whether he ought to send to London for the Amati he had not played since his father fell ill.

He dreamed of her, not just in his bed but in his life—walking beside the lake, in his library, at dinner, in Town—and would often awake distressed because, so often, she was hidden from him in rooms he could not find, or in houses whose address he had lost or never known.

He had read of such things and thought them only poetic abstractions fit for women and sentimental fools. Now he was living those poems, and he hated it. He did not know whether he wanted merely to bed her or whether he wanted to marry her, but he did know both were impossible.

Her mother arrived, witless and improper, still trying to fix his interest on Jane, a sweet girl who quite obviously wanted nothing to do with him and to whom Bingley was beginning to pay a disquieting amount of attention. Her younger sisters had come too—vapid, untaught, and deeply stupid. He imagined them in his home, running screaming through the halls, and felt vaguely sick.

"You are a Darcy, Fitzwilliam. Never forget your duty to that name. What I want, what you want are nothing. Duty is everything."

She was sitting opposite, pale and embarrassed, and he thought he had never loved anyone so much.

CHAPTER 6

WHAT HAPPENED IN THE MARKETPLACE

Two days later, he was sent word that Matthew Walker had died of an infection of the blood. There were rules about that sort of thing, so he rode to see the man's mother in her hovel.

Her neighbours were standing around outside, silent and watchful, while inside the woman wailed her grief. There was little enough he could do, but what there was, he did. He spoke to her brother, ignoring the man's own rage. Twelve children she had borne, and this had been her last. He undertook to pay her a small yearly sum by way of pension. Walker had been promised a job, and would probably have helped his mother as she grew older. Then he spoke to the rector about the funeral and the grave. He had seen too many poor families beggar themselves to pay for a 'proper' funeral. When he left the rectory, he could still hear her in the distance, howling like a dog as they laid him out.

Bingley came to meet him in the town, and together they

rode back towards Netherfield. His hands were sweating inside his gloves, and he felt presumptuous and useless.

Then, as they passed through the marketplace, he saw her, surrounded by her sisters and accompanied by some sweating oaf in a shovel hat, conversing with a group of militia officers. And there *he* was, swaggering in his regimentals, his little tin sword by his side. Wickham, hat in hand, all smiling loath-someness, talking to Elizabeth.

Suddenly, it was there, the anger he need no longer restrain, boiling through him, body and soul. He saw the man begin to form his usual defiant smirk and was off his horse and amidst them before he knew what he was doing. The smirk vanished; Wickham backed away, his eyes wide with alarm, his hands coming up in front of him.

Someone said, "Mr Darcy!" as, with a single blow, he backhanded the swine off his feet and into the gutter. There were voices in the background, but they sounded distant, and he ignored them. He bent down, lifted the man to his feet and pinned him effortlessly against the nearest wall. "I've been looking for you, Wickham," he said, and he did not even recognise his own voice.

Bingley grabbed his arm. "Darcy," he said, urgently. "Are you challenging the man?"

He laughed without amusement, and his eyes never left Wickham's suddenly pallid face. "Don't be ridiculous. Duelling is for gentlemen. His sort is horsewhipped." Someone was plucking at his arm, one of the officers; he shook the puppy free. "You are going to run, Wickham. You are going to run hard and far. I paid your debts in Derbyshire and Cambridge—how long do you think it will take me to get a tipstaff here? And once you are in the Fleet, I will make sure you rot there. So, desertion or a debtors' prison—the choice is yours."

He dropped Wickham like so much filth and turned to the crowd that had gathered. He raised his voice. "Do not lend this man money, and do not game with him: he recognises neither debts nor debts of honour. Do not leave your wives, your daughters, or your female servants around him: he has neither honour nor scruples."

Nobody spoke. They could hear the noise of the two fine horses stamping their feet and snorting in the silence. He turned to Miss Elizabeth and her companions and raised his hat. "Ladies, please allow Bingley and me to escort you home. It seems the streets here are not safe for gentlewomen." They curtseyed, shocked into silence, and prepared to leave with him.

Behind them, the shopkeeper, beside whose wall this had all occurred, called out in consternation. "Sir! Sir! He owes me money! What should I do?"

Darcy turned. "How much?"

"One pound, fourteen and six."

Darcy threw him some coins. "Pass the word. That was the last debt of Wickham's I shall ever pay." He strode off, and the rest of the company had to run to keep up. His face was white and set, and they were all, including the gentlemen, more than a little afraid of him.

Eventually, it was Miss Elizabeth who dared to say, "Sir, we cannot keep up with you."

He looked down at her, and it seemed to them all that he awoke from some unpleasant dream. He stopped dead, blinking. He passed a hand over his face and tried to speak. "My apologies, Miss Elizabeth. I…" He swallowed hard. "You…"

Bingley took over smoothly. "What my friend means is that, now we have left the town, there is no longer quite the same need to hurry." They continued at a more moderate pace. Darcy was shivering now and looked ill. Even Lydia and Kitty were silent for the whole journey and ran into the house as soon as it was in sight.

The sweating fat man looked desperate to follow them, and after hovering beside the rest of the party for a few moments, muttered something about escorting his young cousins and ran off as fast as his legs would carry him.

Elizabeth and Jane were scarcely less shocked than their sisters but, having met the two remaining gentlemen more often and under happier circumstances, were perhaps less afraid. "You must come into the house, Mr Darcy," said Elizabeth. "I fear you are unwell."

He shook his head and she realised that, for the first time in their acquaintance, he could not look her in the eye. "I must beg your pardon, Miss Bennet, Miss Elizabeth, for that most ungentlemanly display. I have never, I should never... Please, apologise for me to the other ladies. It was unforgivable. Assure your father that I shall call upon him as soon as possible to explain myself."

They tried to reassure him but were unsure whether he had understood. Eventually, they were obliged to go indoors.

Elizabeth ran upstairs to her mother's chamber, which overlooked the front of the house. Lydia and Kitty were already regaling her with the details as best they could amidst her noisy flutterings and exclamations. Elizabeth ignored her mother to run to the window.

From this vantage point, she could see over the walls to the road beyond. The two gentlemen had not mounted their horses; indeed, Mr Darcy was sitting on a milestone at the edge of the road with his head in his hands. Mr Bingley stood beside him, bending low to talk. She watched in an agony of indecision, wondering whether to offer her assistance or whether that would merely increase his evident humiliation.

After a few minutes, however, Mr Darcy took his friend's arm and levered himself to his feet. He stood for a few minutes, his head bent, leaning on Mr Bingley until that gentleman clasped his hands and threw his friend up into his saddle. He then mounted himself, using the milestone as a mounting block, and together they cantered off in the direction of Netherfield.

The next day, Mr Bennet was not at all surprised to receive a visit from Mr Darcy. His daughters' many and various descriptions of the previous day's events had whetted his appetite for something truly recherché, a welcome addition to his burgeoning collection of his neighbours' faults and follies.

What he received was a pale, grave young man buttoned to the throat in a black coat who refused both tea and something stronger. He merely sat, turning his hat over and over between his hands, rubbing the nap first one way and then the other.

"No doubt, your daughters have described what happened yesterday." He did not wait for a reply. "I came to tender my apologies to the ladies and to you for my deplorable behaviour. I also feel I ought to extend a warning in case Wickham, despite my...actions, returns. I cannot feel it likely, but it is possible."

"Are you sure you will not take something to drink? You do not look well." This was not at all amusing; it was even a little frightening. Mr Darcy was quite the most important person Mr Bennet had ever dealt with, and despite his usual sangfroid, he was more than a little intimidated.

"I thank you, no. As I was saying, Wickham's father was my late father's steward. Indeed my father stood godfather to him. He was a lively and engaging child, and my father was fond of him, paid for his education at both school and university, and left him...substantial provision under his will. This was squandered as anyone who had known him at Cambridge could have predicted. He had already demonstrated by this time a vicious want of principle that he concealed from my father but could not hope to hide from someone so very nearly his own age. Having wasted his legacy, he demanded more and was both intemperate and abusive when I, not unnaturally I think, refused." He was addressing a point somewhere over Mr Bennet's left shoulder and that gentleman could not help wondering whether Mr Darcy was speaking to him or to himself.

"There was no further contact with him for a number of years although I understand he used my name to obtain both credit and entry into society for which his own merits would have been grossly inadequate. He next came to my attention last year when he suborned a member of my staff in order to gain access to my fifteen-year-old sister, to whom he made indecent advances. His object was undoubtedly her fortune, which is considerable, although I cannot but think that the desire to be revenged against myself provided an additional incentive."

"Mr Darcy," said Mr Bennet when he had finished speaking. "Although I am honoured by your confidence, I am uncertain why you should believe it necessary."

The dark eyes turned to him then with an expression of astonishment. "I thought that, as the father of young ladies, you would wish to know of any threat to their welfare."

"You believe him to be so dangerous? After all, my daughters have no splendid fortune to entice such a man."

"My estate is currently supporting three of his natural children. There may well be more. Not all of them were born to serving maids and the like. Yes, I believe he is that dangerous." And still he turned his hat, over and over. "I hope that this explanation will, in some slight measure, excuse my deplorable behaviour yesterday. I have taken the liberty of purchasing some small gifts for the ladies to express my apologies." He laid a little pile of books on Mr Bennet's desk. "I understand from Miss Elizabeth that you do not object to your daughters reading novels. The two books for Miss Catherine and Miss Lydia are entertaining but entirely unobjectionable. I have indeed purchased copies of both for my sister."

"Will you not stay and give them to the girls yourself? They are currently visiting their Aunt Philips but will return within the hour."

"I preferI prefer not to if you do not mind. The memory of my actions…"

Mr Bennet's patience, never very extensive, was rapidly reaching its end. "Come come, Mr Darcy. You lost your temper. It is hardly the 'sin against the Holy Ghost'."

"Perhaps not, but neither was it the conduct of a gentleman. I cannot think about it without abhorrence. I am leaving

Netherfield today. I hope that the memory of my actions will not long outlast my departure."

He rose to his feet, and Mr Bennet was obliged to do likewise. "Shall we see you at Netherfield again?"

"I doubt it," said Mr Darcy. "Certainly not this year. I have business to attend to, and then I must spend Christmas with my sister at our aunt and uncle's." There was a knock at the library door, and his head whipped round, but it was only the butler relaying word from his coachman that the horses were becoming restive. He closed his eyes for an instant, swallowed hard, and then turned to Mr Bennet to take his leave.

That gentleman, however, had something further to say as he held out his hand. "Mr Darcy, I am old enough to be your father, so I am going to give you some advice. Like most advice from old men like me to young men like you, it will probably be ignored, but I am going to give it anyway. Attention to business is admirable, and attention to the dictates of propriety only slightly less so, but neither will, of themselves, make you happy."

"I have never considered happiness to be a necessary consequence of performing one's duty."

"Perhaps not, but unhappiness is not necessarily a consequence either. It is all too easy to believe that unpleasant actions are one's duty, merely because they are unpleasant and not because they need to be undertaken."

Mr Darcy looked at him for a moment, and Mr Bennet wondered whether he had entirely understood. Apart from anything else, the man looked exhausted. But they bowed and shook hands, and he watched as the younger man climbed heavily into his carriage and departed.

When this departure was discussed by the assembled matrons of Meryton, it was agreed that Mr Darcy was a great loss to dear Mr Bingley, that gentlemen of his active benevolence were not met every day, and (Mrs Bennet being absent that day) that he had somehow managed to escape that lady's plans for her Jane and was much to be congratulated on that account. They also agreed that 'that Mr Wickham' was obviously no better than he ought to be and that they were glad to see the back of him.

The only thing that puzzled the ladies was Mr Darcy's purchase, immediately before he left, of three jars of bottled cherries from Mr Hooper, the pastry-cook.

When Mr Bennet examined the little pile of beautifully bound books, he too was a little surprised. The novels for his two youngest were, perhaps, two of the only books he could conceive of them actually reading, and for Mary there was a recent commentary on the Psalms, considered primarily as poetry. He thought he would quite like to read that one himself. For Jane, Mr Darcy had obviously observed her fondness for flowers, and her gift was a beautifully illustrated botany of English garden flowers—and for his Lizzy? Oddly, this was the only book that had not been purchased new. The book-plate inside the front cover read, 'Ex Libris: Fitzwilliam Darcy, Esq.' It was Wordsworth's *Lyrical Ballads*.

CHAPTER 7

FRIENDS AND
RELATIONS

THE ROADS NORTH OF WATFORD WERE TRULY APPALLING, HEAVY
rain having created a thick, clinging mud that bogged down
the carriage and exhausted the horses. It took him three days
to reach his destination in the hills above Buxton, and he
arrived cold and tired.

He was, however, pleasantly surprised by the house, a large
stone-built cottage, so-called by courtesy only since it was
considerably larger and in better condition than he had
thought from the name. The carriage sweep outside was small
but perfectly adequate for a man as adept as Tom Coachman,
and he climbed out and walked a few paces to stretch his
cramped limbs as Lawson and Hopkins saw to his luggage.

The front door opened before he had a chance to knock.
"Good evening, Bridger," he said. "How is his lordship?"

"Not as well as he was yesterday but better than he'll be
tomorrow, sir. He's waiting for you upstairs, first room on the
right."

He took the stairs two at a time and knocked. Dicky Meopham was propped up on pillows, waiting to see him. He looked as bad as Darcy had expected but not as bad as he had feared although he was very thin and his skin looked almost translucent. "Fitz! Come in, come in, it's good to see you, man!" They shook hands, Meopham's soft and pale against the hard, brown hands of his friend. "I expected you yesterday. Sit down and tell me all your news!"

Darcy lifted a solid wooden chair from against the wall; he did not trust the spindly little thing near the bed. "Vile roads, viler weather, and I hit Wickham in a marketplace in Hertford-shire. Unless you wish me to discuss our prospects in Portugal, I do not think I have anything—"

"You did what?" Meopham struggled to sit up. "You finally gave the bugger his dues and I wasn't even there to witness it?" He started to cough, and Darcy helped him to lie back down, handing him a cordial from the bedside table. "Details—I want details!"

Bridger came in with coffee as Darcy shared the story with his friend. "I cannot believe even you feel guilty about hitting the man," said Meopham. "He should have been beaten hourly since birth." His voice was getting hoarse, but his eyes were still alight.

Darcy sighed and accepted a glass of brandy. "I have no regrets about Wickham, but to lose my temper so thoroughly in public and in front of ladies…"

"Ha! That's nothing to what Wickham would have done in front of ladies, given half a chance." They grinned at one another companionably.

Darcy knew he had to ask, no matter how little he wanted to. "Dicky, do I take it the mercury treatment did not work?"

"'It couldn't. Turns out I'm not poxed after all." Darcy leaned forward eagerly, but his friend shook his head. "No such luck, Fitz. I have a cancer; it's eating me away from the inside."

"Is there nothing that can be done?"

"No, and to tell the truth, I don't much mind any more. It hurts, Fitz. It hurts like the ██████ I'll be glad when it's over."

They sat in silence in the gathering gloom. The lamps had not been lit, and the only light was from the roaring fire. "I am so very sorry, Dicky. Is there nothing I can do?"

"Not now, but I am glad you came. Look, there's some things I have to do. Bridger will be here in a few minutes. You go clean up. We don't dress for dinner or anything silly like that. It'll just be trays on our knees and another chance to talk."

Lawson was waiting for him with hot water and clean clothes. The room was warm and clean but hardly luxurious. He washed and shaved, trying to think of something—anything—he could do for his friend.

Dinner was an excellent beef stew followed by cherry pie, of which even Meopham ate heartily. "So, what were you doing in Hertfordshire?"

"Charley Bingley has leased an estate there. I went down to advise him. I think he'll do well. He has certainly made himself popular with the locals."

"Ah, let me guess. He went to all the parties and danced with all the pretty girls, and you stood round the outside, scowling like the Ancient Mariner. No, worse—you don't even stoppeth one in three."

"That, Dicky, is mere hyperbole." Darcy pronounced it 'high-per-bowl,' and they both laughed

"What was that poor man's name?"

"I don't think we ever knew," replied Darcy. "Everyone called him Sock-rates, even Professor McMicheals." He leaned forward to fill their glasses, and his face came into the lamp-light properly for the first time.

Meopham seized his arm, shocked. "Good heavens, man. You look worse than I do, and I'm dying! Are you ill?"

Darcy shook his head and sat down, heavily. "No, I assure you I am quite well. I am just so very tired. I promise you I am well. I have no right to be unwell. I just cannot sleep."

"Here, pass me that damned cordial, and tell me about it.

Perhaps I can help. Heaven knows you've helped me enough over the years. What do you mean, you 'have no right to be unwell'?"

There was a long pause, and then the words came, tumbling over themselves. "I have a life of ease and plenty, and thousands of men without half my education or fortune lead lives of happy usefulness. It must be self-indulgent—it must! To lie awake, night after night, my thoughts like clouds of flies in my brain, and then to drag through each day, longing for it to end." Darcy got up to pace. "I try to do my duty, but there is no satisfaction in it. I try to be active and useful. But what am I but a walking purse? My father always said, 'Benevolence requires careful thought, Fitzwilliam, not emotion'. Why isn't that enough for me?"

"Because you are not your father, Fitz. Don't forget: I knew him. He was benevolent by rote. If he were you, I'd get a present of game in season and a letter once a month, two sides, not crossed. He'd never have remembered how much I like cherries and The Newgate Calendar. He was a cold-hearted, mechanical sort of man, and if you're trying to make yourself like him, it's no wonder you look so damned ill." He waved his arm in the direction of his friend and the lid of his cordial went flying across the room.

Darcy went over and picked it up, and when he got back, his friend handed him his brandy glass. "Here, drink this, and get yourself off to bed. I've got to dose myself for the rest of the night. We'll talk in the morning." He shook Darcy by the arm. "You're a good man, Fitz. One of the best I've ever met. That's no cause for unhappiness that I can see."

Darcy drained his glass and bade his friend goodnight. For once, he thought he might actually sleep. He did not recall returning to his room; indeed, he knew no more until he awoke the next day, astonished to find that it was almost noon.

He lay for a moment, blinking and trying to clear his head, then he rang for Lawson who brought coffee and shaving water.

By the time he went down and knocked on Dicky's door,

he felt halfway human. "I don't know how you can read these things," he said as he took up his seat near the bed.

"How else am I going to know all the gory details of Captain McNamara's duel or Hatfield, the Keswick imposter?" said Meopham reasonably. "You look better. How did you sleep?"

"Apart from the sensation that my teeth had their own little waistcoats, excellently. What did you give me?"

"A few drops of my laudanum—and don't look like that. I know you. You can be trusted not to make a habit of it." He started to cough, his whole body shaking, and Bridger hurried in and administered various liquids until the spasms died down and he was sent off for more coffee.

"Is there truly nothing I can do for you, Dicky?"

"Actually, there is. I've made you executor of my will. This place belongs to me. It's not part of the entail, and I've left it to you to deal with."

"What about your family?"

"Father's still drinking himself to death, and my revolting brother is just hanging round waiting for one or both of us to die so he can get his hands on whatever's left."

"And your sister?"

Meopham sighed, which started the cough again. "Once they realised I wasn't poxed, that Friday-faced, canting Methody she married allowed her to visit me—once. She only married him because Father said she must and because she knew he wasn't a drunkard or a gamester. Turns out, he's nothing but a cheese-paring pinchpenny. Anything I left her would go in his pockets and never come out. He's one of those fat, gasping, purple-faced men, and she should outlast him. I know I can trust you to see she gets it. If she doesn't, her daughter can have it. Pretty little thing—looks like our mother. There's enough income from it to keep them in reasonable comfort."

Darcy took Meopham's hand in his. "I will see to it. I promise."

"And promise you won't go adding to it because you feel sorry for them. That's not why I asked you."

"Very well, I promise that too."

"Can you keep an eye on Bridger for me? I can't bear this much longer. It won't be long before I take too much of that stuff and just slip away. I hope it gets taken for an accident, but if it doesn't—make sure he doesn't get blamed, will you? I've left him a little money, and you know what kind of mind my brother has."

"Anything, Dicky, you know that."

"Oh-ho, there's a dangerous promise. Very well, I want you to find a pretty girl and dance with her. I want you to do three things you enjoy every day, and I want you to let yourself enjoy them. I want you to tell your relations to mind their own businesses, and I want you to find someone to talk to. Your trouble is, there's no one in your life to tell you when you're behaving like a gudgeon."

"I am beginning to regret making those prom—" began Darcy in mock offence, but Meopham interrupted.

"No, you're not. You're a good man, Fitz. You'll do your best for me. I know that. You always have, ever since I tore the seat out of my breeches climbing over the college walls after lock-up and you saved me from the proctor."

"I had to. I bet Walsingham five guineas you wouldn't get sent down before Christmas."

Meopham struggled into a more upright position, his eyes sparking. "I thought it was pure altruism."

"Well, perhaps not pure."

"This from the man who ran the Dean's drawers up the flagpole. That was you, wasn't it? I've always wondered, how on earth did you get hold of them?"

Darcy lent back in his chair. "Well, there was a housemaid…"

"You didn't!"

"Certainly not! She had three teeth and hadn't bathed since the Gordon Riots. Ten bob and half a pound of marchpane and up the flagpole they went. The best of it was, they suspected Wickham!"

They both roared with laughter and passed the day in reminiscence, interspersed with an excellent steak, cherry tarts, and the last of Meopham's good brandy. When he took his leave the next day, Darcy knew he would never see his friend again.

He knew he ought to go to Alfreton House; it was only two weeks to Christmas, and he was expected, but he knew he had insufficient control of his temper to listen to his uncle Matlock complaining that he would not join in the enclosure of Lambton Common, so he went back to Pemberley.

As usual, Mrs Reynolds was touchingly glad to see him, his apartments were warm and quiet, and all the little news of the estate was good. Mrs Wallace of Glebe Farm had given birth to a healthy little girl, despite her age, and when he called round with the customary gifts, he found the whole family, including her older brothers who were nearly men, besotted with the infant. He had always assumed he would have children one day, but the sight of the crumpled little face in a lace bonnet touched something inside him, and he was, perhaps, more effusive in his congratulations than was his custom. He left, pleasantly warmed by the farmer's sloe gin and christening cake and determined to go and collect his sister a few days early so that they could make the Christmas rounds together.

Unfortunately, however, Darcy was delayed by the continuing terrible weather, and he did not arrive at Summerbridge Hall until the twenty-first of December, cursing his height after a long, uncomfortable coach ride. Georgiana was with Lady Eleanor when he arrived, but Mrs Annesley asked for a few moments of his time before he saw his sister.

Darcy greatly esteemed his sister's companion as a sensible, well-bred, educated woman whose warm personality would, he hoped, help his sister to overcome the disappointments of the previous summer. However, as they took up their seats in a small and unnecessarily shabby parlour, he saw that the lady looked distinctly embarrassed.

"I thought perhaps I ought to warn you, sir," she began.

Darcy was immediately worried. "Is something wrong with my sister?"

"No, sir, not quite. However, I regret to inform you that Lady Eleanor has been unusually and, I might almost say brutally, frank with your sister about..." She blushed deeply. "A woman's...um...marital obligations. I have endeavoured to present a happier and, I believe, more accurate picture, but I fear your sister was greatly alarmed."

Darcy could have cursed. Were all his decisions to go so terribly wrong?

"In addition, I believe that certain, quite kindly meant, comments by Lord Summerbridge about the great match she would be expected to make have quite overset her equanimity. You may find that her behaviour is once more that of a young girl, rather than that of the young woman she was becoming. I do believe this is mere reaction; however, it might be as well not to press her on such matters as her coming out, at least for the time being."

Not for the first time, Darcy wished his mother were still alive. He had had very little to do with very young ladies and, while he loved his sister dearly, often felt that inexperience. He turned to Mrs Annesley. "What do you recommend I should do?"

"Indulge this new fancy for a few weeks. She is a very unassuming girl, and you need not fear spoiling her. If you have no other obligations, I believe she might appreciate some time spent with you." This last was said a little timidly, and Darcy realised she half expected him to refuse. "Moreover, I have had some difficulty in inducing her to continue her practices in the modern languages and the exercises left for her by Monsieur Dupont. On the other hand, her interest in and command of mathematics is such that I cannot even understand her conversation on the subject. If you would like her to continue her studies in this area, it will be necessary to engage a special master. Since I understand you excelled in the same subject at Cambridge, that might form a suitable area for conversation."

The door opened, and Georgiana came in quietly. Without thinking, he strode over and engulfed her in his arms, lifting her off her feet. After a heartbreakingly long, shocked pause, she returned the embrace, hanging on to him almost desperately. Mrs Annesley slipped out of the room unnoticed.

"I have missed you, Georgie," he said, and she blushed with pleasure.

"Truly, Brother?"

"Truly, sweetheart. And you have grown again. I can see we shall have to visit the dressmakers once more."

He took her arm and led her to a sofa. "I have been thinking. We are engaged with Lord Matlock for Christmas. What say you and I make it a short visit and then go to London? Just we two. We shall go to the theatre and to concerts. We could even go to Astley's and the pantomime if you like. We shall not be home to anyone, and if we do not want to go out, we shall stay at home, drink chocolate, and play backgammon."

She threw her arms round his neck. "Oh, could we? Could we really?"

"I do not see why not. And what is more, a very wise man told me I ought to find a pretty girl to dance with. Will you dance with your old brother at Lord Matlock's Christmas party? It will only be the family and a few neighbours."

She was flushed with pleasure, and for the first time, he could see what a beautiful woman she would become once the awkwardness of youth had passed. "I thought you hated dancing."

"No, I do not mind the dancing. It is the conversation I cannot abide." He assumed a simpering falsetto. "Oh, Mr Darcy, ain't we having prodigiously fine weather?"

Georgiana giggled happily. "I promise I shall only discuss Cartesian geometry."

That made him laugh, and he resolved to search out some

of his old Cambridge books as soon as possible. He had always enjoyed mathematics; perhaps it was a family trait.

"Georgie," he said, taking her hand in his. "I know I've been rather low in spirits recently. Something in your last few letters has made me wonder whether you do not perhaps blame yourself." She tried to slip her hand from his, but he held on to it.

"I do not know why I have been like this, but it has nothing to do with you." Without realising it, his voice softened into the Derbyshire burr of Nanny Grayson. "You are very dear to me, Georgie m'duck, and you deserve all the love I can give you."

To his horror, her eyes filled with tears, but as she cried into his shoulder, he understood that he had somehow said the right thing. He held on to her until she borrowed his handkerchief, dried her eyes, and went to get ready for the trip to Alfreton, only a few miles away.

As he swathed himself in coat and shawls, Darcy felt that, for once, he had succeeded. And it was so simple: a little time together, which he knew he would also enjoy, and a little reassurance. His mood lifted somewhat, and as Georgiana's trunk was loaded and she climbed in next to him, he resolved to include her in more of his life.

Christmas at Alfreton was its usual ordeal. Although they both recognised the genuine kindness behind the invitation, the formality of the proceedings was quite beyond what even Darcy thought necessary. The men retired after dinner and drank execrable port—the earl having no taste for wine—and repeated the same opinions to each other that they had been exchanging all day. The earl's attempt to change Darcy's mind about Lambton Common having been rebuffed with unusual firmness, even that subject for debate was foreclosed. The countess, a colourless woman with no conversation, presided over the ladies with a well-bred hauteur that effectively killed all attempts at liveliness and reduced poor Georgiana to a matching silence.

Both brother and sister left in the New Year with some of

the same sensations as children escaping school for the holi-days. They had a travelling backgammon board, and they played the game all the way to London with the sort of laughing ruthlessness only possible between brother and sister.

Darcy House had been prepared for them, and all was warm and inviting. There was also a pile of correspondence waiting for him, which he forced himself to sort through. The only letter that caught his attention was a characteristically ill-written missive from Charles Bingley, announcing his engage-ment to Jane Bennet. "Ah well, too late to do anything about it now," he thought. "He could have done so much better."

Everyone would have to make the best of the match, so he wrote Bingley a short letter of congratulation and settled down to give his sister an enjoyable stay in London. There were a surprising number of diversions to be had for the time of year. They went to concerts of the Academy of Ancient Music where they were introduced to works of the great Elizabethan composers. They went to the Tower of London and saw the Crown Jewels, they went to Astley's Amphitheatre for the circus, and they even went to the pantomime at the Theatre Royal to see the great clown Grimaldi.

It was that evening, in a box with his sister, that he saw *her* again. She was sitting in one of the lower boxes with her sister, an older couple, and a number of wide-eyed children. They were all laughing heartily, and he struggled to take his eyes off her. Beside him, Georgiana, too, was laughing with delight, and he tried to watch the antics on stage and join in her mirth, but sooner or later, his gaze was drawn back to *her*. The days when he could detect any flaw in her were long gone, and it seemed to him that she shone in the candlelight.

His gaze was so fixed that, eventually, Georgiana touched his arm. "Do you know those people, Brother?"

He forced himself to answer calmly. "I believe so. The fair-haired young lady is Charles Bingley's intended, and the other young lady, her sister. I do not know the rest of the party."

There they left it. He prepared excuses for why he did not want to go and speak to them, but they were unnecessary.

Georgiana was still too shy to suggest making new acquaintances. He felt more than slightly foolish, but he could not meet her—not here, not now. At the end of the piece, he waited until the family were collecting the children's hats and coats and, knowing how long this would take, made haste to leave. Sitting next to Georgiana in the carriage, his skin felt tight, and he was hot and uncomfortable. Thank heaven he had no idea where she was staying in London. He did not trust the strength of mind he had always relied on.

CHAPTER 8

ENCOUNTERS IN A DRAWING ROOM

THE VERY NEXT MORNING, BINGLEY WAS ANNOUNCED, bouncing into the library like a retriever pup Darcy had once owned that insisted on bringing him his boots, wagging its tail and grinning proudly. "I got your note this morning," said Bingley, sitting down and then standing up immediately to pace round the room. "I had no idea you were back in London. You must come and see my beautiful Jane with me."

It was all for nothing, and he felt again the sense of inevitability he had felt at Netherfield. It did not matter what he did, he was bound to meet her. He could not refuse; he did not even want to refuse, not even when he found that they were staying in Cheapside with Mrs Bennet's brother and his family. Luckily, Georgiana was at her pianoforte, and he did not have to explain in front of Bingley why she could not join them.

They rode to Gracechurch Street, and Darcy found that their destination was a modest but prosperous-looking establishment with its own yard and a stable hand who looked as though he knew what he was about. There was nothing about the house, its staff, or its inhabitants that he could use to buttress his resolve. Mrs Gardiner was a well-bred gentlewoman who dealt with their arrival with an aplomb that spoke of either innate good manners or experience of good society. The house united taste and just enough fashion as was seemly for the family's position in life.

Elizabeth was sitting in the neat little parlour with her sister and two little girls, whom they seemed to be teaching to stitch. Curtseys and bows were exchanged, and the little girls came forward, confident in their expectations of sugarplums from Mr Bingley, who was obviously a family favourite.

Darcy said the usual civil commonplaces, offering his congratulations to Miss Bennet who, he was forced to admit, was a modest young woman of sense and manners and would probably have done very well for Bingley if it were not for her lack of fortune and her unfortunate connexions. He could see Elizabeth out of the corner of his eye as he spoke to her sister, and he felt as though a jug of warm water had been poured over his head, heat crawling over his scalp and down his back.

He gathered from the conversation around him that Jane Bennet had come for a long-arranged visit, which had been combined with shopping for her trousseau, and that her sister had come with her when their mother had succumbed to a heavy cold. Unspoken between all parties was the general relief that Mr Bennet had insisted the trip not be postponed.

Darcy had no idea what else he could trust himself to say, especially once he recalled that the last time he had seen Elizabeth and her sister had been the day he forgot himself in the marketplace at Meryton. He took up a seat opposite her and watched her with the children. One of the little girls had lost her needle, and there was a little laughing fuss made of looking for it before they both picked up their samplers and left with the nursery maid.

Miss Bennet and Bingley were sitting together making sheep's eyes at each other and were no help at all in sustaining conversation. When Elizabeth came and sat next to him, he was so surprised that he almost recoiled. "I must thank you, Mr Darcy," she said, "for our books. How did you know how very much I wanted to read that particular collection of verse?"

He looked at his hands. "I noticed that you were reading it that night at Netherfield when I was writing letters and the others were playing cards."

He glanced up into her face and watched, fascinated, as she blushed. "And it was particularly gracious of you to give me your own copy."

He had to say something. "After my behaviour in the marketplace, it was the least I could—"

She put her hand on his sleeve. "My father gave us to understand that there was more to your actions than appeared on the surface. I am sure I speak for my sisters when I say that, insofar as forgiveness is necessary, you may be assured of ours."

Two inches further down and she would have touched the skin of his wrist. He hardly heard what she said for the sight of her hand on the green wool of his coat. For a moment, he could only think of how delicate her kindness was, how beautiful that little hand.

She seemed not to notice his lack of speech, for she took back her hand and exclaimed, "And there is the missing needle!" She knelt at her aunt's feet and plucked it from the carpet before tucking it into her own sleeve. "I was always losing my needle when I was a child, and what is more, I am determined my cousins' samplers will not be the sorry failure mine was." He managed to force out an enquiry, and she said, "I laboured for weeks over an alphabet sampler, and presented it proudly to my papa who pointed out what not one of us had noticed: that I had entirely omitted the letter Q." She laughed. "I tried to persuade everyone that I thought Q was an ugly letter, and that 'queen' should be written with a K, but I do not think anyone believed me."

Miss Bennet looked up at this. "And you told everyone the cow in my sampler had five legs."

"It did!"

"That was its tail, as well you know."

Mr Gardiner came in and was just as pleasant and well-bred as his wife, with nothing of the shop about him. Tea was served, and the fortunate discovery that Mrs Gardiner had spent much of her early life in Lambton served to carry the conversation forward. She must still have had correspondents there for she and her husband knew that he had prevented the enclosure of Lambton Common and were gently complimentary. Elizabeth was sitting beside her uncle, her eyes shining, and his heart lurched as he realised she approved.

He tried to think of a way to turn aside the compliment without sounding self-righteous, but his thoughts tangled, and he had to hope they took his silence for modesty. He drank his tea and listened to Elizabeth and her family discussing their evening at the theatre. When Mr Gardiner asked him a question, he had to admit, to himself at least, that he had heard no voice but hers.

He managed some sort of answer and was at once pained and relieved when Bingley announced he had to go. He retrieved his hat and greatcoat, and they made their goodbyes. He thought Bingley a little ridiculous in his effusions; however, the moment he bent over Elizabeth's hand himself, he knew his own struggle was over. He had lost himself as completely as any other poor fool.

As they rode away, he gave in completely. He would marry her, and the relief of that decision was like dropping a heavy weight. He knew he would be failing in his duty, but he no longer cared so long as he had her by his side.

After all, he could make damn sure they had nothing to do with her appalling mother and those two—no three—appalling sisters. He knew she would be relieved about that.

He slept well for the first time in what felt like weeks. He arose early; he was shaved with particular care and dressed in his finest. Georgiana was to spend the day with Mrs Annesley, shopping for the kind of feminine fripperies he was perfectly happy to pay for but had no wish to supervise. Unusually for January in London, the weather was crisp and fine and, as he mounted his horse, he could have sung.

As he left the stable yard, he noticed his cousin Colonel Fitzwilliam climbing the front steps of Darcy House and stopped to greet him. Despite what the newspapers had described as a harrowing campaign season, he looked fit and well, and Darcy was glad to see him.

"I have a call to make," he said happily as they shook hands. "You go in and see Georgie, and we'll talk when I get back."

Fitzwilliam looked up at him. "You look done up to the nines. Where are you going?"

Suleiman was restive, so Darcy contented himself with an enigmatic smile and cantered off to Gracechurch Street.

It was only ten o'clock, so he went round to the family jewellers and arranged for some pieces to be taken out of store and cleaned. When he arrived at the Gardiners' house, it was a little after eleven in the forenoon, a little early by fashionable standards but not so much so as to be impolite. The maid who answered the door took his card and then let him into the same sitting room as before where Mrs Gardiner sat with Elizabeth, both of them sewing something evidently not for gentlemen's eyes for the items were swiftly packed away.

He made the usual civil enquiries after Mr Gardiner and Jane, who were both apparently at the bootmaker's, Mr Bingley being expected during the afternoon. Mrs Gardiner ordered tea, and she was just pouring his cup when there was a loud thud immediately above their heads and the sound of a child roaring lustily with pain. With a muttered apology—it seemed the nursery maid was acting as Jane's attendant that day—Mrs Gardiner left the room.

Elizabeth looked up at where he was standing and smiled. "I am afraid my cousin James is not afraid of anything and has recently discovered the climbing possibilities represented by his bedroom furniture. Last night I had to rescue him from the top of the armoire for, having ascended, he could not work out how to reverse the procedure."

He hardly heard her. All he knew was that they were alone and that he loved her. He strode over to where she sat and stood over her. "In vain have I struggled. It will not do. My feelings will not be repressed. You must allow me to tell you how ardently I admire and love you." He saw her eyes widen; obviously she had not expected his proposal, but once started he could not stop. "From the first, I admired your courage. I soon came to admire your wit, your charm, and your beauty. When you came to nurse your sister, I learned to love your compassion and to crave the loving attention you bestowed upon her.

"I have tried not to love you. The inferiority of your fortune and connexions represent the reverse of what I was taught was my duty to my name and position, but I can no longer struggle against the force of my passion. I beg you to marry me and allow me to take you away forever from the meanness of your current situation and the impropriety of your family. Allow me to give you the life and situation you deserve and in which you are destined to shine."

She was looking at him, her brows knitted, and for the life of him, he could not understand why she remained silent. "I realise," he continued. "That this change in your situation might be difficult, and I have no doubt that there will be those in my family and in wider society who will condemn my choice, but I no longer care. I no longer struggle. I love you, Elizabeth, and will never allow anyone to insult or demean you."

"Except, apparently, yourself," she replied heatedly.

"I beg your pardon?" His heart was pounding, and there was a sudden, strange burning sensation in the small of his back. He felt anger brewing and smothered it as best he could.

"Pray tell me, sir, for how long and how much have you struggled? You imply that you liked me against your will, reason, and even character."

"Did you not hear me say I have set those scruples aside?"

"That may well be the case, but you still feel them in all their force. How can I possibly accept a man who so obviously despises my family and friends? I realise that a woman in my position is not expected to refuse a gentleman in yours, but I have always resolved to marry for love or, failing that, at least for respect and esteem. You say you love me, but it is obvious to me that you neither know nor respect me if you can talk of those I love with such disdain."

Dear God, she had refused him! It had never occurred to him that she might, and he found he had nothing to say as she continued. "At our first meeting, I thought you all that was admirable and benevolent. I thought your silence at the assembly was merely the embarrassment of a modest man receiving applause for doing his duty. I never realised the extent to which you must have despised the company."

"Would you rather I had lied?"

"Sir, I would rather you had never spoken of this at all," she cried, and he saw that she was close to tears. He had to get out; the urge to run as he had not run since he was a boy suddenly gripped him. He seized his hat and bowed, conscious that he was behaving like a spoilt child denied a treat but unable to stop himself.

"In which case, madam, I should withdraw. Pray accept my best wishes for your future happiness."

The stable hand brought his horse, and he started the long ride back to his house. She had refused him. He would have to live the rest of his life without her. She had refused him, and he could have given her so much, not just gowns, jewels, and things he knew she would enjoy but did not crave, but the life of the mind. All the things she had had to scrape together for herself in that dull little town—the books, the music, the theatre—and all the things she had never had but so much deserved: the travel, the absence of material cares, the peace and quiet. The reins dug into his hands, and he realised dully that he had left his gloves behind. She had refused him! How was he to live without her?

Young Tom came out to take Suleiman and was obviously

about to say something about the ride and, equally obviously, decided to hold his tongue. As Darcy entered the house, he thought that perhaps he ought to feel angry. Who was she to refuse him? But the thought seemed to come and go, and there was no anger in him—only a strange numbness.

Fitzwilliam was waiting in the library, and he did his best to rouse himself. The colonel had come back to England to form another battalion to his regiment after hideous casualties in Portugal and Spain. This was a man who had suffered true loss, and Darcy did his best to react appropriately.

The colonel, however, was no fool. He took one look at his cousin, grasped his arm, and led him to a chair. "Good heavens, man. Whatever has happened?" He hurried over to the tantalus, brought back a glass of brandy, and thrust it into Darcy's hand.

It was no use. He had to tell someone, and what had Meopham said? *"Find yourself someone to call you a gudgeon when you need it."* He took a hefty swallow of the brandy. "I have just made an offer of marriage and been refused."

"You were refused? Who did you offer for—Princess Mary?"

"No. I believe I have just been refused by the only woman in England who did not consider my fortune first and foremost." He looked into his glass, and although he did not know it, he was rocking backwards and forwards slightly in his chair.

"She must have been mad. You're a catch most women would give their eye teeth for."

"No, no she was not. Young perhaps but not mad." He swallowed hard. "I made her cry. I proposed marriage and I made her cry. I am no longer sure of anything, least of all my own conduct. Perhaps she was right to refuse me." Fitzwilliam almost protested, but in the end, he said nothing, and they sat for a long moment in silence.

"What are you going to do?"

Darcy shook his head. "I don't know, Cousin. I really do not know. I have to think, and I cannot do that here. Will you look after Georgie for me for a few days? Tell her I have urgent business at home. I shall not be more than a week, and I do not want to worry her."

He set the entire house by the ears, demanding his coach and setting off for Derbyshire within the hour. For he knew he had to leave before the numbness wore away. He was horribly afraid he might weep.

CHAPTER 9

STRUGGLES WITHIN AND WITHOUT

It was a bright clear night, the full moon and heavy frost making for excellent travelling conditions. He did not get out when the horses were changed, fearing to display his reddened eyes. The burning urge to get home at any cost filled his brain, and he had to prevent himself urging the driver on faster than was safe.

The weather changed as they passed into Derbyshire. Rain fell in torrents, slowing the horses and affecting even the surface of the turnpike. After an hour, he brought Young Tom and Hopkins inside, drenched and freezing, and and they were so embarrassed to be there that he pretended to fall asleep. Pretence faded into truth, and he awoke with a start as thunder and lightning split the sky.

In the early light of dawn, he could see that they were in the park at Pemberley—nearly home. They clattered over the bridge to the house, and to his shock, the stream and lake outside were nearly empty despite the rain that, here at least, had obviously been falling for days.

He leapt out and hurried into the house. In the great hall, Mrs Reynolds was supervising the household staff as they carried the contents of the ground floor upstairs. The garden workers were carrying the outdoor statuary indoors and setting it down close to the walls.

"Oh, sir, I am main glad you're back," she exclaimed, hurrying forward.

He took her hand in his. "What on earth is going on outside?"

"The river is blocked at Lambton Bridge, there's a fallen tree across it, and all the rubbish swept downstream has piled up behind it. Last we heard, half the town is underwater, and the river is backed up as far as Kympton."

"Where is Mr Empson?" It was his job to take care of these things after all.

"He was hurt with the men trying to move the tree. He's still unconscious upstairs."

Darcy stood for a moment, thinking hard. The bridge crossed the river at its narrowest point for miles as it passed into a limestone gorge. If they could clear that, then the rest of the town and the lands upstream would be cleared, but downstream it would be like Noah's flood until it got into the water meadows, which would contain most of it.

He glanced around and took charge. Two of the gardeners were dispatched to the Henderson and Wallace farms to warn the tenants of what would be coming down. Truth was, they probably expected it, but better to be sure. A groom was sent even further to warn Mr Pattinson, the next landowner downstream; the water meadows were his, and he ought not to have anything on them, but Darcy did not know him well enough to be certain.

He changed quickly into a heavy, waterproof cloak and stout boots and ordered up Titan, the largest, calmest horse in the stable. As he mounted, he called to Mrs Reynolds. "Get the pensioners out of the cottages. Put them in the guest bedrooms for now. Hot food and a tot of rum for everyone who wants one."

He would not even have attempted to reach Lambton on any other horse. It was still raining heavily, thunder rolled at intervals, and he could see lightning on the hilltops. Lambton was in chaos, the water was still rising, and people were trying to save themselves and their household goods. As he rode down Bridge Street, he saw Mrs Goody, the seamstress, trapped in her bedroom, the water filling her shop and lapping up the stairs. Her son was trying to erect a ladder, but there was a powerful undertow, and he could not make it steady. Darcy rode beneath the window, reached up, and lifted her out, depositing her in her son's arms. She was crying and shaking, and they had to pry her fingers from his coat.

All through the town, the scene was the same. At the bridge, he saw the problem for himself. A huge elm was jammed up against the central pier of the stone bridge, its roots exposed. Behind the tree, branches, dead animals and even a broken farm cart formed a near-perfect dam. Men with grappling hooks were trying and failing to remove much of the debris against the pull of the current. One brave soul had even tried to chop the tree in half from underneath the bridge but had been dragged away by his family.

There was only one thing to be done, and the townspeople were only too glad for someone to tell them what that was. He sent two men to the quarry for blasting powder and fuses and ordered everyone else indoors—some to the church and some to the Royal George, according to their inclination in times of peril. The men came back with one of the quarrymen, and under his expert direction, the charge was set under the bridge by the pier.

The explosion, when it came, was like the wrath of God. Darcy felt the ground lift under his feet. There was an almighty roar, then debris pattered and thudded all around. It later transpired that, thanks to the judicious placing of the powder, very little of it went upward, most of it being blown sideways and into the water. The roar of the river took several minutes to decline to its usual level and then, as the house-holders came out to see what damage had been done, he had to see to the construction of a temporary wooden bridge since half the town was desperate to see what had happened to the other half.

He sent for builders and workmen from Pemberley to help with the immediate needs. They told him his home was safe, apart from some water in the cellars. The houses where the water had entered were full of stinking mud, and he laboured beside his men, shovelling it out and carrying it away to be used on the fields.

When his gloves wore away and the palms of his hands started to bleed, they took him aside, tended to his hurts and sent him home with expressions of shy gratitude he did his best to accept graciously. As he rode back through the woods in the gathering dark, he could barely remain upright in the saddle.

The stream and lake at Pemberley were back to a level only slightly higher than normal, though the state of the gardens revealed the size of the torrent that must have swept through them. As he stumbled into the great hall, he found it full of furniture from the servants' dining room. Exhausted men and women sat slumped on the wooden chairs and settles. The kitchen maids were doling out something hot and appetising from a great cauldron boiling in the fireplace he had not seen alight since before his father died.

The stairs looked mountainous, and he dropped into the butler's high-backed chair that stood beside the fire and accepted a bowl of something halfway between stew and soup. Suddenly, he was ravenous, and he emptied the bowl in a matter of seconds. His clothes were steaming, and he watched the vapour rise for a few minutes. Someone took the bowl from him, and he was asleep almost immediately.

He did not know how long he slept, but he jerked awake when someone sitting behind him dropped a tankard.

"I tell ye, it could 'ave been a lot worser." It was the voice of Granddad Dickin, former head gardener. Officially pensioned off to one of the cottages, he still insisted on walking the grounds every day, telling his son Young Dickin how to do his job.

"'Ow?" came an indignant voice. "'Ow could it have been worse?" That was...um...Hollin, a footman and son of a small farmer near Kympton. He must have had word of the damage.

"Could 'av been t'owd mester Darcy and not the lad. That miserable bugger would never 'ave got 'is boots wet. And I'll tell ye summat else, e'd never 'ave gone round to see for hisself what the damage were. Not 'im! E'd 'ave waited for yon Wickham to tell 'im and ye never knew 'ow much were being passed on, like."

There was a murmur of agreement.

"Come on Dad, time tha' wor in bed." It was Young Dickin, come to find his father.

"Ow's my cottage?" There were sounds of the old man being helped to his feet.

"Bit o' mud on t'floor, we'll get it all cleared out for thee tomorrow."

"I'll nivver manage all them stairs!"

"Never you mind. Hollin and me'll give thee a hand up."

In the great mirror over the fireplace, he could see the two younger men carrying the old one upstairs. He tried to think about what he had just heard but he was too tired. Lawson arrived and helped him off with his coat and boots, and slowly he made his way up to bed.

CHAPTER 10

FACING THE TRUTH

THE NEXT FEW DAYS WERE FILLED WITH BUSINESS. RAIN WAS still falling, and he returned every night drenched to the bone and exhausted. His house was still at sixes and sevens, the cellars needed to be drained, and the gardens were just muddy meadows with stumps of shrubs and trees showing where years of work had disappeared in minutes. He got used to sharing his study with the eight-foot-tall statue of Circe and the Swine that his grandfather had brought back from the Grand Tour.

Eventually, order at Pemberley at least returned, and he had never appreciated Mrs Reynolds and the servants more. He still had to ride out to supervise the essential repairs. Empson was too injured to help, so he rode the estate alone. He did not want to notice how astonished people were to see him, but he could not avoid it. The tenants and townspeople, although deeply grateful, were undoubtedly surprised to see him in person and seemed to grow more astounded the more he talked to them.

He had plenty of time to think as he crossed and re-crossed the land, and he could not help but remember all that astonishment. There was Mrs Goody's son shaking his hand in tears in the marketplace—"Oo'd 'ave thought it would be thee, mester!"—and the Wallaces' surprise when he had congratulated them on the birth of little Maria before Christmas, Mrs Annesley's fear that he would not want to spend time with his sister, and Georgiana's shock when he embraced her. Dear God, what had he become? What had he made of himself?

And Elizabeth, shocked and in tears in the Gardiners' sitting room—had he considered her at all? He claimed to love her but had never taken the trouble to discover her feelings. Why should she feel *anything* for him? Had he bothered to show *her* anything but the most superficial aspects of his character? Then he had insulted her family; and when you came down to it, what was wrong with them? Her mother was silly and grasping, but she was only silly because no one had taught her and grasping because she was afraid. The younger sisters were giddy and improper to various degrees, but they were young and could learn. He burned with shame that he had not remembered to exempt Miss Bennet from his strictures. Elizabeth and he could have sorted everything out between themselves—he knew they could—and he would not now be so alone, trying to work out what best to do for the concerns of dozens of people without anyone to tell him when he was being a gudgeon.

He knew Dicky did not want him to visit so near his end, but he would have given much to be able to tell him how right he had been about everything.

Pattinson turned up to thank him for the warning. Apparently, the man was ass enough to have had stock on the water meadow although his extreme youth could not but excuse him. Darcy cursed to himself as he realised that Old Mr Pattinson must have died and he had never even noticed. He invited the young man for something to eat and drink before he went back to his own estate and saw Pattinson's surprise at the invitation.

So he made the effort to talk to him and found a youngster

eager to do the right thing and not at all sure what it was. He could not leave the lad at such a loss, so he offered to ride down the next day and see whether there was anything he would advise. More surprise, decently covered, as the offer was eagerly accepted.

That was another reproach. When had he last tried to disguise his feelings before those he considered his inferiors? If he was displeased, he made no effort to hide it. He had always thought Bingley was joking when he referred to leaving him alone to contemplate his own virtue. Obviously, it was not a joke—or not entirely.

As he struggled to help people back to their homes and work, he tried to sort it out in his own mind. He knew he was not a bad man; the people of his own household were content, and they obviously respected him and appreciated his efforts on their behalf. He was notably charitable to those in need. But beyond that? When had he started to believe everyone was beneath any consideration save that of master or benefactor?

"You are a Darcy, never forget that," his father had always said. But what did that mean? What ought it to mean? He knew he no longer wanted to be the man his father had been, so who did he want to be?

Pattinson was grateful and eager to learn, so he spent a couple of days with him, learning to like the boy along the way. He lent him some books on agricultural practice and made enquiries for a steward for him. His estate was too small to need one most of the time, but as Pattinson himself agreed, he needed someone to teach him his business.

A man came from the turnpike company to discuss the new bridge. He was tempted to send him off with a flea in his ear—what was he supposed to have done, let the town drown? But a second look revealed a man sweating with fear. Heaven only knew what he was expecting from the man who had blown up the company's bridge. He was tempted to refuse to pay any part of it and make them sue him for every penny. If they had built the damn thing properly, there would have been no problem. But he reined himself in, offering to pay half and provide the stone if they built it without a central pier. Judging by the man's agreement, he could have got away with half as much, but he knew that, at least this way, the town would be sorted out as soon as the weather permitted and there would be work for some of the local men during the winter.

And always there was Elizabeth, in his thoughts and in his dreams. He knew she would have done better than his clumsy efforts to help people. She would have known how to persuade the Widow Hinchcliffe out of her cottage until it could be repaired. She would have known what to give Mrs Wallace to replace the things the baby needed and had lost in the flood. She would have known what to say when he came home covered in mud and discouraged by how much there was still to do.

The house felt damp, and he ordered coal fires to be lit in all the rooms—hang the expense.

Fortune and connexions? He did not spend the money he had; what did he need more for? And what sort of connexions could he offer her? Lord Matlock, dimly conscientious by his own lights. Aunt Augusta, preoccupied with society and the manifold shortcomings of her acquaintance? Summerbridge, all selfish religiosity? Lady Catherine and Anne—one a domineering, old harridan and the other a bundle of shawls who said little and did less, poor thing. Really, apart from Fitzwilliam and Georgiana, he had no one to whom he could introduce her with pride.

So what if society disapproved? He loathed society, over-heated scrummages full of people he disliked with concerns he did not share. They could have made a society of their own of intelligent, conversable people who did things worth discussing —people, he realised with a sinking feeling, like Mr and Mrs Gardiner.

He knew he had come to this knowledge of himself too late. He had lost her, and sometimes that fact was almost more than he could bear. However, there were people who relied on him, more than he had ever realised before the flood, and he had a duty to them and to her—a duty to become the sort of man she could respect.

As the crisis trailed to an end, he remembered Dicky's words. God willing, he had a long life in front of him; he had better learn how to live it properly. He made himself call on his neighbours. One or two were self-important or illiberal, one was a disgusting drunkard, but most were decent gentle-folk who were pleased to see him. Jack Pattinson rode over once a week and became a real friend.

He dug out the fiddle he kept at home and forced rusty fingers to remember their old skill. He was surprised at the pleasure he got from it. And he was not the only one; more than once, he caught maids or footmen pausing in their work to listen. He had most of the contents of his father's study moved into storage and made the room into an annex of the library, filling it with pictures of summer scenes and flowers.

There were days when talking to people was more effort than he wanted to expend, but he made himself continue, gradually coming to appreciate the comfort and companion-ship. He often found himself without anything much to say but decided ruefully that he would have to be content with being known as 'reserved.' He just hoped people added, 'but polite.'

Georgiana's letters became more insistent, so he allowed her to come home, now the worst of the damage had been repaired. She wept when she saw the gardens but soon settled down to help him with the visiting, becoming ever more comfortable in his company. One day she actually disagreed with him.

It was not the life he wanted, but it was a good life, and he made himself remember that whenever the memories became too painful and sleep deserted him.

He was so busy that it was not until Fitzwilliam wrote to remind him that he remembered their yearly visit to Rosings was only a week away.

CHAPTER 11

EASTER AT ROSINGS

He left for London the next day, after teasing Georgiana that it was time she took up her share of family responsibilities and came to Rosings too. He had written to his cousin to meet him at Darcy House and was eating breakfast when Fitzwilliam arrived with a pile of newspapers and a merry cry of, "Hail to the modern Guy Fawkes!"

Darcy looked up from his bacon. "I beg your pardon."

Fitzwilliam helped himself liberally to breakfast and nodded towards the newspapers. "News of your exploits has spread, Cousin. I saved those for you, although I must say, if I had never been to Lambton, I'd have thought you'd demolished some towering edifice over a mighty, foaming torrent." He laughed happily as Darcy groaned. "Horatius Cocles—only backwards," he added, proving to his cousin that at least some of the money spent on his education had not been wasted.

"So, ready for another three weeks of terrible dinners and

afternoons spent persuading Lady Catherine's tenants not to flee for the hills? I take it you are going to let her exploit you shamefully again this year?"

"Of course I am," answered Darcy distractedly as he read the papers, trying to find some resemblance between what he read and what had actually happened. "If I don't, I shall have to spend the afternoons talking to her and not just the evenings."

Fitzwilliam stared at him. "That is brilliant!"

"I know, and I thought of it first, so hands off!" He threw the paper away with a snort of disgust. "I hope no one I know will believe any of that rubbish," he said, resuming his breakfast. "Firstly, I am not stupid enough to set the charges when there was an expert workman there, and secondly, you will be pleased to hear that the stained glass of St Luke's is intact." He watched as his cousin reached for the coffee pot. "How's the shoulder?"

"Very well, thank you."

Darcy lowered his eyebrows and, in his best Nanny Grayson voice, said, "Nah then, Mester Henry, tell the truth and shame the ██████!"

Fitzwilliam grinned unwillingly. "It aches and stiffens up in the cold weather, but I can use it well enough for active duty when the regiment goes back to Portugal."

Darcy nodded and resolved to keep an eye on him. They could always stop when they changed horses if his cousin looked to be in pain. "I ought to warn you," he said. "This visit might be more than usually unpleasant. I plan to talk to Anne and then tell Lady Catherine that I shall not marry her. It isn't fair to Anne to keep this hanging over our heads, and we both know how Lady Catherine is going to react to that." He finished his breakfast and looked up to see his cousin looking at him with a curious expression.

"You have changed," said Fitzwilliam slowly.

Darcy shrugged. "I think there was room for it, don't you?" he said lightly.

Despite their secret hopes, they arrived at Rosings in time

for dinner although neither of them felt ready for the seven overdressed courses their aunt thought appropriate. Neither were they looking forward to the guests they were told to expect. Darcy had not met his aunt's new parson but, remembering the last one, refused to hope for a sensible man.

The water for washing came in a ridiculously ornate silver ewer, which ensured that the water was only tepid. His room smelt musty, and there was dust on the windowsill; his aunt had never had any idea of how to run a household, and her housekeeper was far too cowed to institute improvements. For the first time ever, he realised what a wretched existence his cousin must have and, although he knew he could never marry her, wondered whether there was anything he could do to make her life more bearable. He would have to think about it carefully.

They gathered in the salon before dinner. He kissed his cousin Anne's cheek when she came down and saw that the mere gesture alarmed her, although Lady Catherine looked worryingly pleased. Then they sat around, listening to their hostess pontificating while they waited for their guests to arrive.

First into the room was the new vicar, Mr Collins—greasy, obsequious, and faintly familiar in appearance—pushing his way in front of his wife, a sensible-looking gentlewoman of seven or eight and twenty with much better manners than those of her husband. She looked familiar too. Was she not from Meryton? Miss Luke? Luker? Miss Lucas—that was it. Poor woman must have married that unctuous idiot of a parson.

Then, to his utter amazement, *she* came into the room: Elizabeth, beautiful in a gown of palest lavender, her cheeks pink with the evening chill. For an instant, he forgot about everyone and everything else. His heart leapt, and a smile of incredulous joy broke over his face until he saw her blush scarlet and look away. Memory was like a dash of cold water in his face. He bowed and did his best to greet them all appropriately. He saw that she was suffused with embarrassment, so he went over to Mr and Mrs Collins to tender his congratulations and be introduced to the girl with them, reluctantly giving Elizabeth his back.

Mr Collins was a severe test of his new resolution to be civil to everyone, but he could see that the man's wife was being made uncomfortable by her husband's compliments to the company, so he did his best to distract him—an activity made more difficult by the recognition that Collins was the fat fool who had been with the Miss Bennets the day of what he now thought of as 'the Wickham incident'. This explained why the man was quite obviously terrified of him and remained so throughout dinner.

Luckily for their mutual peace of mind, he was not seated near Elizabeth although he could hear her talking to Fitzwilliam and Lady Catherine. Even as he made polite conversation with Mrs Collins and Miss Lucas—enquiring after mutual acquaintances in Hertfordshire and agreeing that Mr Bingley and Miss Bennet were a particularly well matched couple and ought to do very well together—he could hear *her* voice, and he rejoiced in her refusal to be overawed by his aunt.

They joined the ladies almost immediately; Collins appeared desperate to get back to safety, and there was music. She seemed uncomfortable in his presence, so ill at ease, but she played and sang as well as ever. He dared not go over to the piano when Fitzwilliam did, so he sat and tried to distract Lady Catherine so she would not interrupt with her usual witless comments. *"If I had ever learnt, I should have been a great proficient."* What on earth was that supposed to mean? His mother, her sister, had learnt, and he had always been told that she was an accomplished musician. He had a sudden vision of his grandfather Matlock sternly ordering one daughter to learn and the other not, and despite the seriousness of the situation, his lips twitched.

He glanced up and saw Elizabeth looking at him, her expression thoughtful beneath all the embarrassment, and knew he would have to talk to her somehow. He had wanted to apologise to her for weeks but had seen no way of doing so without intruding into her life and making things worse for her at home. He might have succeeded in feeling more charitable towards her family, but he was under no illusion as to her mother's probable reaction to the news that she had refused him.

However, they were both expected to stay in Kent for some weeks, and he did not wish her to remain unhappy in his presence, nor did he wish to ruin her visit with her friend. He would apologise and then, if she wished him to, he would leave. It was the least he could do.

His original intention had been to walk in the park near the parsonage, hoping to meet Elizabeth since he knew she favoured early morning walks. However, the first of his aunt's tenants arrived before breakfast, and there was a steady stream of tenants, villagers, and work people all day. One poor man, a thatcher, reduced to abject poverty by Lady Catherine's failure to pay her bills, was so incoherent with the anger he dare not express to a member of the gentry that he had brought the vicar's wife to speak for him, thereby reaffirming Darcy's initial impression that she was a sensible, well-intentioned woman who was far too good for the man she had married.

That evening only the family were present, and thus the conversation was much less pleasant and involved far fewer people; Lady Catherine held forth and the rest of them made variously successful pretences at listening to her. Darcy could see his cousin Anne withdraw into herself, and he wondered what she was thinking. He hoped that she was not imagining married life with him since, before he left Rosings, he would have to kill that particular daydream. Even if he had not proposed to Elizabeth, he knew he could never have married Anne. That way lay happiness for no one except, perhaps, Lady Catherine.

The next day was more of the same as word got round that grievances and outstanding accounts were being met, for to do Lady Catherine some little justice, she never objected to the decisions he made. He sat in the library—adjudicating, settling, placating—and it seemed to him that some of the complaints were so petty that, for the first time, he wondered whether she deliberately ignored her responsibilities in order to tie him to Rosings with bonds of obligation to those she neglected. Or was that too Machiavellian even for her?

The constant demands on his time and attention severely affected his patience, and had it not been for his violin, he might well have completely lost his temper with his aunt, if not with her dependents. Luckily, she heard him practising on the first afternoon—in the brief period between the last petitioner and dinner—and demanded entertainment in the drawing room. So, that evening, he did his best to lose himself in his music, and if he occasionally played rustic songs of Derbyshire in the style of the London Bach, he suspected only Fitzwilliam noticed.

He was finally free of obligations on a day when the Collins party was invited for the evening. He made arrangements to be woken at dawn, shaved close, and—despite all the self-knowledge he had so painfully acquired over recent weeks—could not help dressing his best. It was only just light when he stepped out into the park. After days with the estate maps, he knew the most likely path for her to take and was waiting for her when she came around a clump of trees, her bonnet in her hand and her face turned up to the rising sun.

He snatched off his hat. "Miss Bennet." He tried not to notice the way her face fell and she instinctively looked behind her for a way to escape. "Please! Do not be alarmed. I am not here to importune you or to ask you to change your mind. I only need a moment of your time, and then I shall leave you to your walk in peace."

He could see she was ready to flee, but she was no coward and turned to face him. "I do not know what you think you have to say to me after our last meeting, but you may speak."

"Thank you." He took a deep breath and ignored the trembling of his hands. "I only wish an opportunity to apologise for my disgraceful and ungentlemanly behaviour at our last meeting." He swallowed convulsively. "I cannot...I do not apologise for my sentiments towards you. However, the way I chose to express them...I cannot think of it without abhorrence. You do not have to say anything, but please know that I deeply regret my conduct. If you wish me to leave Kent for your ease and comfort, I am yours to command."

Whatever she had expected, it had obviously not been this. She coloured, looked down, and there was a long pause until, eventually, she spoke. "I cannot deny, sir, that I was greatly shocked by your manner of declaration." He could see her twisting the ribbon of her bonnet and longed to put a hand over hers to stop her. "However," she continued. "I accept your apology, and I do not believe that it will be necessary for you to leave your family party." She looked up at him from beneath her eyelashes. "I understand from Lady Catherine that you only visit once a year. I am unwilling to force you to lose the many pleasures your visit so obviously affords you and the colonel."

He bowed. "Justice tempered with mercy. Pardon and penance in one sentence."

"Come, come, Mr Darcy," she said, obviously desiring to lighten the moment. "Despite Lady Catherine's strictures, I do not believe my playing is so very bad."

"Actually, Miss Bennet, I was referring to *my* playing, and you will have ample opportunity to judge that this evening." She smiled at that, and he felt himself flush like a boy and did not care. "I shall leave you to your walk and look forward to seeing you at dinner."

"Mr Darcy." She curtseyed.

"Miss Bennet. Good day and, once again, my thanks." He bowed and they parted to go their separate ways. If she had looked behind her, she would have seen the sedate and genteel Mr Darcy jump up to swing on a low branch, knocking off his hat in the process.

Dinner was, for Darcy at least, a much more comfortable affair than any during his stay in Kent. He decided against sitting next to her; he had her forgiveness, not her affection, but from where he was sitting, he could include her in his conversation occasionally, which meant much to him. When he played at his aunt's request, although she did not realise as much, he played to her, and when she smiled, he could feel the joy rippling down his fingers and into the strings.

The next day, he permitted himself to meet her briefly on her walk, just long enough to exchange civilities. She was cautious, perhaps even a little alarmed, so he made himself avoid a meeting the following day.

The day after that was Sunday. He had to sit in the family pew with Lady Catherine, Anne, and Fitzwilliam, which meant he could not see Elizabeth. He thought he could hear her singing, but he could not be sure, no matter how hard he listened. Mr Collins's sermon surpassed even the previous incumbent's for sheer fatuity. The idiot appeared to believe that 'ye have the poor always with ye' was some form of commandment and not the reproach Darcy had always taken it to be. Luckily, Collins was still afraid of him, and when he spotted Darcy frowning at him, the sermon came to an abrupt and incoherent end.

Outside, while Lady Catherine was berating the luckless cleric for failing to improve upon the text she had given him, Darcy took the opportunity to exchange a few words with Elizabeth. She looked enchanting, and he had to force himself to think of something complimentary but not presumptuous. Fitzwilliam was at his elbow and was bound to say something if he did not, so he settled on, "The spring sunshine seems to suit you, Miss Bennet. How are you this morning?"

"Very well, sir, but disappointed not to hear you sing. Obviously, Rosings' serpent player and violinist are in more accord than ours at home in Hertfordshire."

"I do not think they would dare be anything else," said Fitzwilliam, and Darcy's heart turned over as he heard her laugh. It was a delightful sound, rather deeper than the high-pitched titter he knew too well from society ladies, and he felt a small, heated kick in his stomach as he heard it. He kept his face as non-committal as he could although inside he reproached himself bitterly. Every day, it seemed that what he had lost through his own stupidity became more obvious and more desirable. His only consolation was that his unhappiness did not appear to be visible to her.

That afternoon he sought an interview with his cousin Anne. Under other circumstances, her heartfelt relief that he was not intending to propose might have been amusing or even insulting. However, he was content to accept it for what it was: the relief of a young lady in poor health who had no desire to enter into the married state with anyone, least of all a cousin she regarded as both more clever and infinitely more active than herself. She only begged the favour that he would not confront her mother until the end of his visit. Despite appearances to the contrary, she was enjoying the company and the change in the stifling routine her mother thought necessary to safeguard her health. Under the circumstances, it was hardly an unreasonable request.

The Collins party were expected for dinner and, after the embarrassment of the afternoon, he gave way to his feelings and engineered a place next to Elizabeth. She did not seem unduly upset, and he laid himself out to be agreeable. As Lady Catherine boomed her views on domestic economy to the apparently grateful Collins, and as the over-seasoned, over-cooked courses succeeded each other, he allowed Elizabeth and Fitzwilliam to tease him about his recent appearance in the newspapers. "I read what they said about me, and I have resolved never to believe more than half of anything I read in the newspapers ever again. I would advise you both to do the same, Fitzwilliam, Miss Bennet."

"Ah yes, Mr Darcy, but which half am I supposed to believe in this instance?"

"Why the heroic, dashing part, of course," said Fitzwilliam.

Darcy glowered at his cousin in mock displeasure. "I suggest, Miss Bennet, you start by disbelieving all the adjectives and dividing all the verbs by at least two. Add in the quarryman who really set the charges and the almost total lack of damage to the town from the explosion, and you should come to a more or less correct picture."

"Correct perhaps, but so much less interesting. You make reading the newspapers sound like a mathematical exercise, and I was never very good at such things. Anything after the twelve times table and the rule of three and I am completely astray."

"Darcy! What are you talking about? Fitzwilliam! I must have my share of the conversation!" Lady Catherine demanded from the end of the table.

"We were talking about the inherent unreliability of the newspapers, ma'am," he replied unwillingly.

"Ghastly, misconceived inventions," said Lady Catherine at her most imperious. "I refuse to have them in the house. Together with the unfortunate mania for educating the lower orders, they only serve to make the lower classes discontented."

Some of the upper classes manage to do that on their own, he thought, and from the expression on Elizabeth's face, something similar had crossed her mind. They exchanged small, shy smiles of recognition as Lady Catherine ordered the ladies to withdraw with an admonition to the gentlemen not to linger over their port.

They did not. For one thing, Lady Catherine knew as little about port as her brother, and the cousins suspected that what they were drinking had been adulterated with heaven-only-knew what. For another, Collins was no company, and while frightening him was entertaining, it was hardly gentlemanly.

Darcy had been ordered to play after dinner, so he tuned up rapidly and began one of his favourite sonatas by the father of the London Bach. Lively and tuneful enough for listeners, it had a mathematical perfection to it that he had always found particularly satisfying.

Elizabeth was sitting behind Mrs Collins, and he could not see her face, but he poured out his feelings in every note. He knew the piece so well, he hardly needed the music, and he let it take him, dropping every defence. It was one of those rare but perfect times when he was the music. He held nothing back, and even Lady Catherine sat silent.

When he finished and they were applauding, he got to his feet so he could see her at last. She was staring at him, brows knit, lips compressed, her face set in stone, and he knew, without a shadow of a doubt, that she hated him.

When next day he received word that Dicky Meopham had died, he was more than glad to go.

CHAPTER 12

NECESSARY ARRANGEMENTS

He met with Lady Catherine as soon as possible the next morning, and the meeting was, in every respect, quite as unpleasant as he had anticipated. Her rage was both unlady-like and extreme. She accused him of everything from lack of familial duty to breaking her daughter's heart. Only his recent understanding of the difficulties of his cousin's life at Rosings prevented him from refuting this as bluntly as she proposed it. He was both furiously angry and exhausted by the time the interview terminated, and it was obvious to him that all connexion between himself and his aunt had been severed for all time unless, unlikely as it appeared to him, she could be brought to apologise for her undignified abuse.

Fitzwilliam had already accepted an engagement with a local acquaintance for that day but agreed quite readily to Darcy taking the coach in which they had both arrived. He could always travel post; campaigning in the Peninsula had held much worse than a hired equipage. He, too, had decided to leave; Lady Catherine's abuse had been heard throughout the house, and he had no wish to stay where his cousin and friend was no longer welcome.

"Will you be a good fellow and call at the parsonage and convey my apologies to the ladies for not taking my leave in person?" Darcy did his best not to sound eager. "I do not wish to call in person in case our aunt gets news of it. She is unlikely to react kindly, and I do not want Mrs Collins in particular to suffer for it."

Fitzwilliam agreed, they shook hands, and Darcy set off on the long journey north. He could not avoid passing the parsonage. Elizabeth was crossing the lane into the park as he passed, and he saw how beautiful and graceful she looked in her shabby old spencer and bonnet. She cut him dead. No, he had not been mistaken the previous night; she hated him. He wondered what had happened between their conversation at dinner and his music. Had he embarrassed her? Had he demonstrated feelings she had no wish to know and was anxious to turn away? He did not know, and although he tried to persuade himself that his situation had not worsened in Kent, he was entirely unsuccessful. Apparently, there were some things that could not be achieved by force of will.

He turned his attention to what awaited him at Meopham's cottage. Bridger's letter, which had followed him from Pemberley, was distressing and urgent. The new Lord Meopham was behaving as badly as his brother had anticipated and, although Darcy had instructed his solicitors to maintain a discreet watch, was already attempting to lay claim to the property before his brother had been buried a week. He regretted bitterly that he had not been informed in time to attend the funeral; there ought to have been someone there who remembered Dicky Meopham with affection.

The two days it took him to arrive honed his anger to a deadly efficacy. The new Lord Meopham met him at the door, unshaven and ineffective, blustering that he would contest the will, that the family had been cheated, and that Darcy must have influenced his brother during his long illness.

This was one occasion where his rage could properly be let loose. He towered over Dicky's worthless brother. "If you dare to challenge me," he said quietly but with unmistakable intent, "I shall ruin you, Meopham. I shall drag the case through Chancery until every penny of the estate has been wasted in costs. Then I shall pursue you personally for every penny you have or ever will have. And what is more, I shall not even notice the expense of your destruction."

Meopham was gone within the hour, abusive but defeated. Darcy spent the next few days sorting out the estate, arranging for Bridger and his wife to stay as caretakers until they decided what to do with their legacy and for the few minor repairs necessary to be undertaken. The property had two farms and a number of cottages as a small estate, so he visited the tenants and made sure they knew the identity of their new landlord.

Then he went to call on Dicky's sister, Mrs Hollernshaw, in Chester. Her husband was an MP and was, he hoped, in London preparing for the new session. According to Dicky, the man was too mean to take his wife to Town. His luck was out and the MP was there, just as fat and unhealthy as Dicky had said. His wife looked tired and was grieving for her brother, a fact that Hollernshaw seemed incapable of recognising. Darcy found himself wondering how many happy marriages there were and whether happiness in marriage was even possible.

He extended his condolences as kindly as he could and gave the lady some books and pictures of Dicky's he thought she might like. She was pathetically grateful although her husband had not the grace to refrain from estimating their value. When Hollernshaw left the room for a moment, Darcy took the opportunity to inform her of the legacy he was holding in trust for her, details of which he had written in a letter he now hid in one of the books. There had been a time when he would have scorned to come between man and wife in this way, but he felt such a terrible compassion for her that the thought of not doing so never crossed his mind.

Then back to Pemberley at last. The gardens were on their way back to something approaching their former glory, the lawns had been reseeded, and boys with rattles had been employed to scare away the birds. Georgiana was glad to see him, but so was everyone else. As his carriage came through Lambton, there were more bows, curtseys, and doffed caps than he ever remembered seeing before. A life with purpose; that was his hope and intention now.

He was so tired that it was a day or two before he attacked the accumulated correspondence of weeks. Empson was up and about, so most of the business letters had been dealt with, but the personal ones lay in a neat pile in his study.

There was one from Bingley. He could not look at that yet. If Elizabeth had told her future brother of their dealings, he would probably have lost one of the few good friends on whom he could count. While Bingley would not have told him when he was being a gudgeon, that day had surely not been far off.

Instead, he turned to the letter from Fitzwilliam, his neat, four-square handwriting unmistakeable.

My Dear Darcy,
This is a damn difficult letter to write since I might be completely astray, but I think you ought to know what transpired in Kent after you left.

When I got back from Greenlay's, I found the house in complete uproar. It appears that Lady Catherine has insulted Miss Bennet in every way possible. According to Mrs Collins, after dinner your last evening at Rosings, while the gentlemen were drinking that nasty stuff she calls port, Lady Catherine informed the ladies that she expected the marriage between you and Anne to come off that summer and 'unite two great estates as their families had always intended.' You know how she talks. Anne was too afraid or too accustomed to letting her mother have her own way to object, and the ladies were forced to offer their congratulations.

81

Then, when you refused to go through with it, our aunt went down to the parsonage and accused Miss Bennet of luring you away from your duty with, well…to put it bluntly, womanly wiles and allurements. I am afraid your interest in the lady was rather obvious. In any event, you can imagine what sort of language our aunt used. She was brought up in a different age when coarse language was usual, and I doubt she has forgotten a word of it.

Mrs Collins says Miss Bennet acquitted herself nobly, refusing to be cowed by the old harridan, denying everything including our aunt's right even to question her about her actions. I did my best to set them both right, and I think I succeeded.

Miss Bennet in particular seemed upset that she had believed Lady Catherine about the marriage. Is she the lady you offered for in London a few months ago? Not my business I know, but it would explain why she looked so angry when we rejoined the ladies after dinner; she must have thought you were leading her on while all the time intending to marry Anne.

I shall be in London for another two weeks with the Regiment. The new recruits are a desperate lot: half of them cannot ride, and the other half do not know one end of a carbine from another. They are far more likely to kill each other than the French. I am staying at Matlock House if you need me.

I hope I haven't over-reached myself with this letter. If I am wrong, just put it down to an old soldier whose finer sensibilities have been coarsened by war.

Your affct. cousin,
Henry Fitzwilliam

Hell and damnation! So that was it! He sat back in his chair, anger and relief at war until relief won. He resisted the urge to order up a horse and gallop for miles for sheer joy. If she did not hate him, then anything was possible. Georgiana was playing in the room opposite, so he went in and requested some happy music and, leaving the doors open, went back to his letters.

As the joyful sounds of Mozart cascaded through the halls and corridors of Pemberley, he opened Bingley's letter. It was an invitation to stand up with him at his wedding in Meryton, only two months away.

CHAPTER 13

RETURN TO NETHERFIELD

HE SAT BACK IN HIS CHAIR, THE LETTER IN HIS HAND, AND DID his best not to let his hopes run away with him. His suit was really no further forward than it had been before Lady Catherine had intervened. If Elizabeth did not hate him, there was no reason to believe that she loved or even liked him. No, the best he could allow himself was that she had seemed to find his company tolerable—which, he reflected wryly, was at once a great advance and a rather pathetic foundation upon which to build his hopes, especially since his relationship with Lady Catherine would do nothing to endear him to her.

He looked back at the invitation. Georgiana was included, and under other circumstances, he would have regarded the occasion as a perfect one to introduce his sister to wider society. A small group of people away from London in a private setting would have seemed ideal. Moreover, the match between Bingley and Miss Bennet might serve to allay some of the fears his sister harboured about marital felicity by showing her two gentle, affectionate people obviously marrying for love.

The disadvantages were twofold. Firstly, Caroline Bingley made Georgiana feel uncomfortable; secondly, the behaviour of Mrs Bennet and the three younger Miss Bennets was almost precisely calculated to alarm a shy girl already terrified of social disgrace.

He mulled over the question all day until, at dinner, the obvious answer occurred to him. He could ask her. The juvenile behaviour he and Mrs Annesley had noted before Christmas had been abandoned on her return to Pemberley as she took up a share of visiting the tenants and their families. Her gentle shyness had proved little barrier to her innate sympathy and kindness. What better way to demonstrate his renewed faith in her judgment?

"We have been invited to Charles Bingley's wedding in Hertfordshire," he said. "Before you decide whether you would like to attend"—he saw her eyes widen at the offer of a choice in the matter—"there are a number of things you should consider. Caroline Bingley will be our hostess, and we both know how she is likely to behave." Brother and sister exchanged glances of understanding, while Mrs Annesley busied herself with her dessert.

"Secondly, the bride's family, well some of them at least, are somewhat raucous and frankly rather ill-bred. I don't believe there is any real wickedness or anything of that nature, but the bride's mother and her three younger sisters are…shall we say, not as ladylike as one might wish. The bride, Miss Jane Bennet, and her sister Miss Elizabeth are charming young ladies whom anyone would be pleased to meet. It is merely the rest of the family who might make you feel uncomfortable. Rest assured: I shall try not to leave you in any situation that makes you uneasy; however, I cannot guarantee it."

Georgiana considered for a moment. "Would I get new gowns for the occasion?" she said guilelessly.

He grinned over the table at her, and Mrs Annesley

seemed startled at what a marked difference it made to his countenance. "Most definitely."

"Then, if you please, I should very much like to attend Mr Bingley's wedding."

The intervening period passed quickly. Intensive work was required on the estate before he could leave it for a protracted stay in Hertfordshire. Jack Pattinson came to dinner one evening and, Darcy was amused to see, was rather taken with Georgiana, who was so much her usual shy self that it was impossible to see whether his interest was reciprocated. He supposed he would have to get used to the idea of his sister having admirers even if, at the moment, they both seemed like children to him.

Then they had to go to London for the promised visit to the dressmakers, both his sister and the usually phlegmatic Mrs Annesley having scorned his suggestion that something might be made locally. Before they left, he went down to the strong room and took out a few items for her from the family jewels, things he had not seen since the days when he had watched through the balusters as his mother went down to one of the grand dinners or balls his father had hated so much and over which, he had always been told, she had presided with such grace. It was time Georgiana began to come into her inheritance.

London was its usual smelly, turbulent self. He pleaded press of business to avoid callers, burying himself in his work to avoid the temptation of rehearsing their eventual meeting in his mind. He had learned the bitter futility of attempting to award roles to other people in the expectation that they would act their parts according to his direction. Mrs Annesley and Georgiana disappeared nearly every day and returned exhausted by whatever arcane practices ladies endured while purchasing their clothing. He affected an air of good-natured, brotherly scorn while entirely ignoring the new coats, shirts, hats, and boots that Lawson was imperturbably packing away in preparation for their stay at Netherfield.

The weather for their trip could not have been better. The roads were in good condition, and a brief rain shower had laid the dust. Mrs Annesley was taking his sister through M. Dupont's exercises in the formation of the preceding direct object in French, and he found himself staring out of the window at the passing scenery, trying and failing not to hope that he would see her as they passed through Meryton. He had never before noticed what any woman wore, but he found himself wondering whether she still had the bonnet with the burgundy-coloured ribbons. He thought what she would look like with the family rubies in her hair and about her throat, and had to open a newspaper on his knees and attempt to read.

If she was in Meryton, he did not see her, and was ridiculously disappointed by that fact. However any thought of Elizabeth was blown from his head by the warmth of Bingley's welcome. He could not help but laugh at the sight of his host attempting to bow to Georgiana, shake his hand, and thank him for his wedding present, all in the same breath.

"Welcome, welcome, Darcy, Miss Darcy, Mrs Annesley. Do come in and meet my dear Jane."

Elizabeth was in the sitting room with her mother and her oldest sister, just preparing to leave. "Not burgundy at all," he thought. "Palest green, faded with washing and so very becoming."

Introductions were made, curtseys exchanged. Georgiana trying to get a word out and distressed by her failure to do so. Elizabeth, self-conscious, not meeting his gaze. Caroline Bingley fawning after him in a dark-red dress that did not suit her, and Mrs Bennet, as shrill and as loud as ever, now with an added satisfaction in her manner.

"Oh, Mr Darcy," she said, bustling up and laying a hand on his arm. "We have just been admiring your wedding present. However much did it cost?"

Surely, she had not just asked him... Over her head, he could see Caroline Bingley looking triumphant and instantly resolved that his own behaviour would be better. He bowed to Mrs Bennet. "I assure you, madam, that mere money cannot express my happiness at my friend's good fortune."

Elizabeth was at her mother's side, pale with mortification, and he longed to reassure her how little it mattered. Bingley and Miss Bennet were engaged in their own adieus and had not even noticed, and neither he nor his sister would repeat the tale. As for Caroline Bingley, she plainly did not favour the match anyway.

He wished Elizabeth would look up so she could see how little affected anyone was, but she kept her head down as she hustled her mother to the door. Apparently, they were due later that evening to dine and must go home to change.

Bingley went out to see his guests off, and they were left alone with Miss Bingley. "You see what I have to put up with!" she said, standing far too close so that, in looking down at her, he was presented with her bony shoulders and chest. "Surely, it is not too late. Cannot something be done about this match?"

"I believe Miss Bennet to be an estimable young lady. I see no reason why anything should be done," he replied, trying to end this conversation before Georgiana was exposed to even more bad manners.

"Yes, yes," she said testily. "But her mother!"

"We can none of us help our relations," he said, thinking of Lady Catherine, and realised too late that she would see this as a reference to her own origins in trade. Luckily, Bingley came in at this point as he wondered how—and indeed whether—he should attempt to explain away that particular comment.

Georgiana elected not to attend dinner even though he spoke to her at some length beforehand. He thought she understood that, while bad manners and ill breeding were to be deplored, it did not excuse bad manners in return. However, although she willingly conceded that perhaps Mrs Bennet was more to be pitied than disdained, she confessed herself unequal to a formal dinner in the presence of so many strangers and elected to dine in her room with Mrs Annesley, who claimed to be tired after the journey.

If Lawson thought his care in dressing for dinner was unusual, he was far too well-trained to say so, while Darcy stood before the mirror, wondering whether his last haircut had left it too short and whether he ought to change his coat.

His indecision ended abruptly when he heard a carriage outside and hurried down to greet the guests. There were rather more than he had anticipated, and as he stood in the doorway of the sitting room, he had to summon up the memory of his recent experiences. Reserved but polite, that was his aim. Perhaps he should make it the family motto: *taciturnitas sed comis*. Or would *reticentia* be better? Recognising the thought as an attempt to delay his entry, he forced himself into the room.

First to come up was Sir William Lucas. He was easy enough; a few comments about his daughter's situation and the esteem in which she was held by her husband's parishioners saw him quite contented. Some of the others were more of a trial, especially those who had read of the Lambton Bridge incident, but he did his best to be civil.

This meant that he had to stand for some time listening to Mrs Philips, who was voluble in her complaints about the rogues and vagabonds she seemed to feel abounded in the local fields and woods. "For someone is stealing all my eggs, and Mrs Long lost an entire beef steak pie, stolen right through the kitchen window under Cook's nose."

Despite this flood of words and his desperate attempt to pay the lady the attention that was her due, he was still instantly conscious of the moment when *she* arrived. She was wearing the lavender-coloured gown she had worn at Rosings, and he could feel himself flush, the sensation of heat as instant as coming into the blacksmith's forge from the cool of an autumn day. He clasped his hands behind his back to hide their trembling and wondered whether every man felt like this in the presence of the woman he loved.

Mrs Philips wandered off in search of more loquacious company, and *she* came over to where he stood. She looked embarrassed but determined, and he had never loved her more.

"Mr Darcy, I feel I must apologise for my mo——"

"My dear Miss Elizabeth," he interrupted gently. "If we start apologising for our relatives, 'which of us shall 'scape whipping'? You have, after all, met Lady Catherine."

"In that case, you must let me apologise on my own behalf. I do not know whether Colonel Fitzwilliam has related our conversation." She looked up at him, and when he nodded, she continued. "Then you know how I misjudged your actions. It was most ungenerous of me. I know you to be a generous and honourable gentleman, and I am ashamed of my lack of judgment and charity."

He had forgotten how tiny she was. Such a little frame to hold so much life, so much courage. "Miss Elizabeth, so long as you believe my intentions now are honourable, I find I do not care how we have misunderstood each other in the past." Was he going too fast? She looked thoughtful but not alarmed or repulsed and, when they were called for dinner, readily took his arm into the dining room.

He had not hoped to be seated next to her for dinner, and he was not. Caroline Bingley's doing no doubt, but he did not care. He had spoken to Elizabeth, and they had parted civilly; after their past dealings, that was so very, very much.

It was, therefore, with considerable good humour that he devoted his conversation to Mr Bennet, who was sitting on his left, succeeding in largely avoiding Miss Bingley on his right who, therefore, found herself trapped in conversation with a particularly ebullient Mrs Bennet.

Mr Bennet apparently preferred his conversation to that of Louisa Hurst, and they managed a civil exchange on the types of ideal society in the writings of Plato and Sir Thomas More. This had the added advantage of entirely excluding Caroline Bingley from their deliberations. He thought he had succeeded in hiding his self-consciousness in the presence of the man he hoped would become his father-in-law, and he was pleased to find him a man of education and sense. Darcy had no illusions about the man's failure to run his household or his family with propriety or prudence, but at least it would be possible to converse on equal terms. He wondered whether it would be possible to lead the older man into a more dutiful attitude towards his own family and then chided himself for, once again, trying to lead another person's life for them. There might be something he could do in the future if, please God, he were to succeed in his suit, but that must be a matter for discussion with Elizabeth. He had much more confidence in her ability to deal with other people than he had in his own. He had made too many mistakes in the past, and they had cost him dearly.

He refused dessert and sat back to examine the diners. There was, he realised, a Bennet daughter missing. The large, noisy one—Lydia, that was the name. Perhaps they had realised she was too young and too ill-behaved to appear in public. On further consideration, he knew that this had never prevented her presence in the past, so he enquired of Mr Bennet.

"I am surprised that you should mourn her absence, Mr Darcy," replied that gentleman. "She is indisposed and has been left at home to make a nuisance of herself there rather than here."

"Nothing serious, I trust." He hoped he kept his displeasure at this manner of address to himself.

"Too many sweetmeats, I expect. Now, as I was saying. I have always thought that Utopia…"

This was, Darcy reflected, typical of the man's interaction with his family. He supposed the fact that Mr Bennet esteemed Elizabeth was a mark in his favour; that he had not thought to arrange a decent future for her by way of dowry, was not. As he listened and nodded, he was conscious of a strange sensation in his chest: part admiration of her courage in refusing a man who could have secured her future and that of her family, part anger that her future was so imperilled. Mr Bennet appeared only a little younger than his own father had been at his death.

When the ladies retired, Darcy did not dare watch her leave, conscious of the gimlet eyes next to him. However, Bingley was anxious to return to his intended bride and, after a little good-natured teasing from his guests, they rejoined the ladies. Elizabeth was seated next to her mother, and as they entered the room, he could see that, once again, she was deeply embarrassed.

Mrs Bennet's shrill tones pierced the air. "I care not who knows it. I still say that you could have secured Mr Collins and then we could be assured of staying at Longbourn when your father dies."

For a moment, he hesitated. Would she be more embarrassed if he approached to change the subject or if he stayed away and let her mother continue?

"I see you are wishing my death upon me once more, Mrs Bennet. Take heart, madam: you may die first."

That did it—his poor love surrounded on all sides by insensitivity and noise. She was lively herself but not in this loud, vulgar way. How she must hate all this. He approached and bowed. "I wonder, Miss Elizabeth, whether I could persuade you to play? I remember with particular pleasure the music you gave us during your stay at Netherfield." The relief on her face was all the reward he required. He followed her over to the fortepiano and wondered whether he dared volunteer to turn the pages. She looked up at him and smiled shyly, and he was seated before he knew what he was about.

She played the first few bars. He could see that her hands were trembling somewhat and, on impulse, upset the sheet music onto the floor. He apologised, loudly enough for the room to hear, and in the bustle of setting matters aright, she had time to compose herself.

"It is very kind of you to bother with a rank amateur such as myself, Mr Darcy. You forget that I have heard you play,"

"I assure you, Miss Elizabeth, that I have always taken great pleasure in your music." He dropped his voice. "Although I would, of course, be delighted to have the opportunity to play a duet." Was that too forward? Apparently not, for although she flushed slightly, she smiled.

"Perhaps our styles of playing would not suit."

Now that was definitely encouraging. "I have already taken considerable pains to make my playing more agreeable to my listeners," he said. "I would be more than happy to make any further adjustments you might consider necessary."

"Perhaps I ought to hear more of your playing before I venture an opinion." She looked up, and he knew that she could see the fond smile that creased his face. "Page, Mr Darcy. It is time to turn the page."

He dare not press the matter further. "My sister has accompanied me for the wedding. I would be most grateful for an opportunity to introduce her to you and Miss Bennet. She is somewhat shy and did not feel equal to a large dinner party; however, if you are available tomorrow or the day after, I would be honoured if you would permit me to make her known to you."

"My sister and I shall be at home tomorrow morning and should be delighted to meet Miss Darcy. I am afraid our afternoons are committed to the dressmaker, the milliner, the shoemaker…" She rolled her eyes, and they laughed quietly together. Elizabeth finished her piece, and was displaced at the instrument by Miss Bingley, who was undoubtedly hoping to secure his services as page-turner.

He was in such good humour that he turned away as though he had not noticed her expectant presence, and exclaimed, "Ah, coffee. May I get you a cup, Miss Elizabeth?"

As they left the fortepiano, she shook her head. "I am afraid that was rather wicked of you, Mr Darcy."

"I know. However, I believe the fox has the right to revenge on the hound. Just once in a while."

"Poor, hunted Mr Darcy."

"You have no idea, Miss Elizabeth. You have no idea." He

passed her a cup of coffee, a little cream, no sugar, and they were separated by the press of company: she to her sister's side, he to Bingley's to discuss the political situation, the war in Spain, the health of their respective families, and the utter and complete perfection of Miss Jane Bennet in face, form, and disposition.

CHAPTER 14

THE FATES OF TWO SISTERS

THE NEXT MORNING AT ELEVEN, DARCY AND GEORGIANA WERE driving towards the gates of Longbourn. The weather continued excellent, and he had borrowed Bingley's curricle; the man had been rooked on the carriage, but the horses were excellent, and they bowled along, seeming to respond to his mood.

Georgiana was nervous but not unduly so as they were announced. The youngest Miss Bennet was not to be seen and neither was her mother, but the other four young ladies were present and rose as they entered. As he had anticipated, it took only a few minutes for the two older sisters to recognise and respond to his sister's shyness, and he was content to sit back and watch as they gently drew her into conversation. He particularly admired the way they set her at ease, asking only such questions as could be answered easily in a few words, so that, at the end of the visit, she felt able to express her congratulations to Miss Bennet at some little length.

They parted with expressions of mutual esteem and pleasure, agreeing to meet on the following Sunday afternoon at Netherfield for music. Elizabeth, with a sly smile in his direction, encouraged Georgiana to recruit him into the party once he confessed that he had brought his violin with him.

Elizabeth came with them to the door, and as he helped his sister into the curricle, she exclaimed, "Please wait a moment, Mr Darcy. I have a pair of your gloves that you left at my uncle Gardiner's house. I shall go and fetch them."

Although he protested his unwillingness to put her to any trouble, he followed her into the house, leaving the Longbourn stable hand at the horses' heads. As she started up the stairs, a great wailing broke out from an upper floor—at least two women's voices, amongst which were the well-known tones of Mrs Bennet.

"Oh, Mr Bennet! Whatever shall we do? We are ruined! And now Mr Bingley will never marry Jane and we shall all be turned out! Oh, Lydia! How could you!"

She turned to him, stricken and alarmed. There was the sound of running feet behind her, and he had time only to seize her hand and whisper, "Whatever it is—I *will* help!" Then he had to leave and drive away before the noise reached his sister and alarmed her.

He hoped it was only Mrs Bennet's propensity for drama at work, but if not, he hoped to God that Elizabeth would trust him enough to confide in him.

There was no way he could ask. Whatever had happened at Longbourn was, so far as good manners and propriety were concerned, none of his business. Without an invitation, he could not even call, for *she* at least would realise his motive for visiting, and he would not have her ascribe it to mere curiosity. That afternoon and the following morning, he rode out, hoping to meet her on one of her walks. He did not, and the anxiety was crushing.

As he returned for a late breakfast, he determined to confide in Bingley and get him to call; surely, whatever it was would not be hidden from him at least. As it turned out, he did not have to make the request; as he ascended the stairs to change, he saw Bingley was in the hall, a letter in his hand, his expression shocked and dismayed.

Darcy grabbed him by the arm and led him into the library before he said anything indiscreet before the servants or, even worse, Caroline Bingley. His host went willingly, apparently stunned.

As soon as the door closed, he turned to Darcy. "It is Jane," he said. "She is releasing me from our engagement. Damn that wretched girl!"

"Who—Jane?" Darcy asked, although he had had his suspicions since yesterday.

"What? Oh no. Lydia. The stupid girl is with child. Someone unsuitable. Jane thinks I shall want to get out of our marriage." Bingley sat down heavily and looked up at his friend. "How could she think that of me, Darcy? She knows I love her."

Darcy handed him a small glass of brandy and watched him down it. "There are plenty of men who would want to be released. You know that."

"But not me."

"No, not you." Bingley was, he recognised, a better man than he himself had been only a very few months ago. "She is doubtless shocked and upset. I rather think women feel this sort of thing more than we do. She merely needs your reassurance."

"She begs me not to come and see her." Bingley waved the letter dejectedly.

"Then go and see her father. Make him understand that you have every intention of fulfilling your obligations. Offer to help with the problem. I have no doubt that Miss Bennet harbours feelings quite as strong as your own. Her offer to release you must be making her feel wretched."

Bingley got to his feet. "You are right, Darcy. I shall go straight away." He smiled. "You are a good friend. Thank you for not trying to persuade me out of the marriage."

"I would never try to persuade you away from happiness.

Oh, and Bingley, do not tell Caroline. All this might still be hushed up."

He had little hope of that. Mrs Bennet was not a woman to keep her family troubles to herself; still, the fewer people who knew the better. Bingley wrung his hand and went to change. Darcy struggled with his conscience for a moment. He could hardly intrude on the family now, but he was so desperate for sight of her that he resolved to ride with his friend as far as the gates of Longbourn—just in case.

And for once, luck was with him. As they arrived, he saw a set of familiar, burgundy-coloured ribbons leaving the path and striking into the woods. He shook hands with his friend, set him off into the house, and dismounting and leading his horse, followed her through the trees.

He had to walk for some way, for she knew where she was going and he did not, but eventually, he found her in a small clearing, sitting on a fallen tree, looking utterly dejected, her bonnet on the ground beside her.

He removed his hat and approached. She rose hurriedly, drying her cheeks on the back of her hand. "Mr Darcy, I did not expect to see you here."

He had no wish to equivocate. "I know everything," he said. "I was with Bingley when he received your sister's letter. I have just left him, going in to speak to your father. If Bingley has any say in the matter the wedding will go ahead."

She sat down so suddenly her teeth clicked together audibly. "I told Jane not to worry, but still, we none of us could help it," she whispered. He handed her his handkerchief, and she dried her eyes. "I have been thinking and thinking what was best to do, and nothing I can devise will do."

"What has been decided about the poor child?"

"We have to decide what to do with Lydia first."

"I am sorry, I meant Miss Lydia. She is of an age with my own sister, and I am afraid I still think of her as a child."

She looked up at him and he could not read her expression. "She will have to go away somewhere—but where? We cannot burden my uncle Gardiner with the disgrace, and we know of nowhere suitable although some place will have to be found."

He could not sit next to her; it felt more intimate than he could aspire to, nor could he kneel, for that held other connotations. So he stood at a little distance, aching to take her in his arms.

"I have a property not far from my home in Derbyshire. A couple act as caretakers, but it is otherwise empty. I could ask my own nurse, who has been complaining of a lack of activity in her retirement, to go there and look after Miss Lydia." He smiled wryly. "She is a kind-hearted woman but not one who is easily persuaded. Miss Lydia would be well looked after, even loved, but not indulged. Once her confinement arrives, her family could join her."

She rose to look at him face to face. "Mr Darcy, that is most generous of you, but I cannot ask you to take our troubles upon yourself."

He could not help himself. "Miss Elizabeth, do you not know? I long to take your troubles upon myself. Not because I wish to place you under any obligation to me but because your pain distresses me greatly."

She put out a hand, and he took it in his. Her expression was wondering. "Still?" she said.

"Still and always, my love." He bent and kissed her hand and felt her start and shiver beneath his lips. "I swore to myself I would not importune you, but I cannot stand by while you are anxious and unhappy. Let me take care of you."

She looked up into his face, searching for something, and it seemed to him that they stood like that for an age. Then she made a soft sound and laid her head on his chest.

He put his arms about her, pressing her to his heart. Suddenly, the world seemed full of light and splendour—the sun on the leaves more bright, the song of the birds more jubilant. His heart was huge in his chest, and he felt close to tears. She was crying softly, and he held her, not caring why she had consented, knowing only that she was his and he was hers.

He had a sudden vision of her at Longbourn, racking her

brains for some solution to a problem that was none of her making and not hers to solve, knowing herself to be the only person with the wit and humanity to come to a proper and generous resolution. He knew that not the least of what he could give her was power—power and choices, the ability to do what needed to be done—not just for herself but for others who were dear to her.

She was speaking, and he had to hold her away from him slightly so that he could hear. "I was so afraid," she said. "I thought that you would go, just when I was coming to know you better."

"I am not that easily got rid of," he said gently, longing to kiss her but wondering whether it was too early. "I shall always be here, as long as God spares me."

She rested her head on his chest again, and he kissed her hair and rested his cheek on it. Her arms crept round his waist, and he thought his heart would burst. He had to fight not to crush her to him, his tiny, valiant love.

To hell with caution. "Elizabeth?"

She raised her head. "Yes?"

"May I kiss you?"

She smiled shyly, and he could not but smile back. "I think I would like that." She looked around and then marched over to the fallen tree. Lifting up her skirts daintily, she stood upon it and beckoned him over. "I fear we are going to spend a lifetime of sore necks—you are so very tall, sir."

"I shall arrange for a selection of footstools in every room," he said as he put his arms round her and bent his head. She was laughing as their lips met.

The poets were right. It was like lightning, a sudden shock that gripped his entire body. She was soft and welcoming, and it felt as though his entire being were concentrated in his lips. She was shy and, he realised with a leaping heart, untutored, but she held nothing back until the moment his tongue slipped between her parted lips.

"Oh!" She drew back and looked at him, a hand to her lips. "The books never mentioned tongues. Is that usual?"

He could not help it. He gave a great shout of laughter and whirled her around off her feet before setting her back on her tree trunk. "Quite usual, I assure you. Why? Did you not like it?"

She looked at him for a moment, her head tilted to one side. "I am not sure. I think further experience is called for." They kissed for long, slow minutes until it was more than either of them could bear and they released one another.

"I must return home. My mother is distracted, and if I am not there to prevent it, I fear she will go into town and share the news with my aunt Philips and, thus, half the county." She shook her head angrily. "I do not understand why she cannot be brought to behave more reasonably." She laid a hand on his arm. "I regret I cannot bring you connexions more to be esteemed."

"I cannot deny that there was a time—we both know there was a time—when such things mattered to me. But I have learned better. You taught me better, dearest, loveliest Elizabeth. I have tried my utmost to change, to become a man more worthy of you."

"I fear you grant me more than I deserve, Mr Darcy."

He gathered her hands in his and pressed them to his heart. "No, I do not. I have not your instinctive generosity, your kindness, nor your interest in other people. But I have learned, and I shall continue to learn from you. As for your mother..." He shrugged. "She is afraid, and that fear has made her unwise. Once you and Jane are settled and her own future less precarious, perhaps she may have less cause for nervous 'alarms and excursions'."

"And Derbyshire is such a very long way away." That was his Elizabeth, generous but not foolishly so.

He smiled and kissed the hands he still held; then he unhitched his horse, and together they walked back to Longbourn.

CHAPTER 15

A SWELL OF HAPPINESS

IT IS A TRUTH UNIVERSALLY ACKNOWLEDGED THAT A YOUNG man whose proposal of marriage has just been accepted must be desirous of an immediate wedding. This was definitely the case with Fitzwilliam Darcy; as they walked back to Longbourn, he was busy with calculations, and it was fortunate that he remembered to consult his intended before they arrived.

They stopped beneath a towering oak. "Dearest," he said. "I am anxious to settle matters between us and your father, but I am not sure this is an appropriate time."

She looked up at him, and it was all he could do not to kiss her again. "I understand your concern," she said. "But surely we need to tell him your suggestion for Lydia?"

"If you think it wise. I do not wish to intrude on your family when feelings must still run high."

They continued on their way as she considered further. "Perhaps we should see whether Mr Bingley is still at Longbourn. If he is still closeted with my father, we can join the...um..."

"Council of war?"

"Indeed." She smiled, threaded her arm through his and leaned her head against his shoulder for just a moment until the uneven ground forced them apart. She clambered down the small bank to the road and waited while he led his horse down. Here on the highway, they had to walk apart, and he felt ludicrously bereft of her touch.

As they walked, they talked, and he was astonished once more at how well their minds matched.

"How is Miss Lydia?"

"Only now coming to realise the extent of her disgrace. To do her justice, she had no idea what he was about until it was too late." She shook her head angrily. "Girls are taught so very little of any use."

"I agree, which is one reason my sister spent very little time at school—a mere ragbag of facts without any rational foundation or scheme. So far, I have been unable to find her a master who is prepared to tutor her in mathematics, despite her earnest desire to learn and considerable aptitude."

"And Lydia has so little curiosity!"

"I have often remarked on how rare a trait that is—in men and women." As they talked, his heart sang. Not for him a wife without conversation or intellect, not for his children a mother who mistook the value of education for sons and daughters, not for them the formal visit to the nursery once a day to see the children scrubbed up and cowed into obedience. He saw the corridors of Pemberley alive with laughter and scampering feet and knew she would teach him how to be the kind of father he wanted to be.

As they walked through the gates, the stable boy ran out, and they discovered from him that Bingley was still at Longbourn. Mr Hill, the butler, was quite obviously disinclined to admit Darcy, but Elizabeth overbore him.

Inside, the house was cool and quiet. "You had better wait here while I speak with my father. I shall not be long." So he stood in the hall, feeling intrusive beneath the swell of his happiness. Elizabeth did not leave him long and, in a few minutes, showed him to the library. She stood on tiptoe to give him a hasty kiss on the cheek before she went upstairs. Darcy watched her until she disappeared around a corner and then knocked.

Darcy's first thought was that Mr Bennet had aged noticeably since last he had seen him; his second was that Bingley had obviously settled his own business to their mutual satisfaction, for they both had half-empty glasses before them. They stood as he entered, and Mr Bennet extended a hand over his desk. "I understand you wish to marry my Lizzy. I believe that is the most sensible thing I have heard anyone say all day."

Darcy did his best to hide his reaction to the comment and merely bowed and took the proffered hand. "Yes, sir," he replied. "And I undertake to do my utmost to make her happy."

"You are aware of our current family difficulties, and yet you still wish to join us? This is taking altruism to positively saintly lengths. I expect no better of this young fellow." He gestured to Bingley, who was still sitting with a remarkably foolish grin on his face. "But I must say, I took you for a man with more care for the family name."

"I do not believe my name will be anything other than greatly enhanced by adding your daughter's to it." He devoutly hoped that would be enough talk of his feelings. "Do I have your consent, sir?"

"Oh certainly, certainly. I would be a fool to refuse it under the circumstances. Especially since I understand from Lizzy that you have a solution to at least part of our problem." He motioned to a chair. "Pray, sit down. I am all ears."

Darcy briefly outlined his proposal, ending, "I can assure you of the discretion and trustworthiness of the couple who currently run the house, and my former nurse, while both kind-hearted and efficient, is not a woman who would take any…um…nonsense."

"So your solution is we pack the girl off to the middle of

nowhere?" Darcy could not see whether Mr Bennet approved or not.

"Not the middle of nowhere. It is not far from my own home, Pemberley, and as my wife, Miss Elizabeth would have the means to visit regularly. If you wish, Mrs Bennet could also visit under pretext of a visit to us. I assure you the house is comfortable and Miss Lydia would not lack for care or medical attention in due course." He looked over the desk and added carefully, "I take it marriage is not an option?"

Mr Bennet shook his head. "This will probably make you take to your heels, but the man is a mere private in the militia, a man of some address and education but totally unable to support a wife, even if army regulations were to allow it." He sighed. "I have had to let him off scot-free. We dare not have the news spreading."

Darcy wondered whether his cousin Fitzwilliam could do more but merely shook his head and said uncomfortably, "How do you propose to keep the secret?"

Mr Bennet apparently understood perfectly because he sat back in his chair and blew out his cheeks. "So far we have given out that Lydia is unwell and that my wife is tending to her and is unable to receive visitors. How long we can keep that up, I do not know. Lydia must go away, of course, for the sake of Mary and Kitty at least, and now we have somewhere safe she can go. All that remains to be decided is how we can explain her absence and persuade my wife to hold her tongue."

Darcy swallowed hard; this was his chance. "Might I suggest, then, that Miss Elizabeth and I marry from Pemberley?" He shrugged. "We proud, rich men are notorious for insisting on our own way. You might say I demanded it. No one will think it amiss if the family all travel to Derbyshire. And no one will comment if Miss Lydia does not return with the rest of the family but remains for an extended visit with her newly married sister." He caught sight of Bingley's face and added, "We could even make it a joint ceremony. Most of Bingley's family are in the North."

His future father-in-law was looking at him with an expression half-amused, half-admiring. "You seem to have worked everything out to your satisfaction."

"Subject, of course, to your approval and Miss Elizabeth's."

"And my wife?"

"I hardly like to say."

"Oh, do." Darcy had a nasty suspicion that Mr Bennet was starting to enjoy himself. Dammit, this was the most uncomfortable conversation he had had since Mr Gardiner's drawing room.

"Perhaps, she might be informed that my marrying your daughter is conditional upon utmost secrecy. I believe we can fill her thoughts with happier matters and give her more suitable subjects for conversation with her neighbours."

Mr Bennet sat back in his chair once more. "That, sir, is the mark of true genius. I fear you are a sad loss to politics."

Darcy repressed the urge to squirm in his chair. "If by that you mean that I show an aptitude for deceit, I must protest. In normal circumstances, anything that smacks of disguise is abhorrent to me. However, in the current situation, I do not see we have any choice."

"Oh no, believe me, I am only too glad to have so elegant a solution to hand. How do you suggest we proceed?"

Darcy took a deep breath and resisted the urge to tug at his neckcloth. This was all for *her*, he reminded himself. "Miss Lydia is thought to be unwell. If she and Mrs Bennet travelled to London, to…consult my family physician, we could announce our engagements and follow in a week or two. After a period there to acquire wedding clothes, we could travel to Derbyshire and be married by special licence."

"Masterly, Mr Darcy, and how do you propose to console Mrs Bennet for the loss of the wedding she has been planning in her head since Jane was first out of leading strings?"

Darcy smiled slightly. "I shall invite my uncle Lord Matlock and cousin Viscount Summerbridge to attend."

"Have a brandy, Mr Darcy, and let us fortify ourselves before we inform Mrs Bennet of the happy news."

Upstairs in their bedroom, Elizabeth poured out her news to a radiant Jane. "And best of all," she said, falling back on the bed, "we can care for Lydia without damage to the family reputation and without cruelty. Do you know what he called her?"

"No."

"'Poor child.'"

Jane came and sat next to her and took her hand. "But, Lizzy, do you love him?"

Elizabeth sat up and embraced her sister. "I hardly know," she said. "But I do know that he is completely to be trusted and that he is gentle and generous and loves me dearly." She sighed. "And, Jane, that is more than I have any right to expect."

Jane, who scarcely believed anyone good enough for her sister, began to protest, but Elizabeth merely laughed and insisted on all the details of Mr Bingley's visit. They were happily engaged in exchanging details of their respective betrothals when a familiar voice was heard from the library.

"Oh, Mr Bennet! What wonderful news! Oh, Jane! Oh, Lizzy! Oh, my nerves!"

CHAPTER 16

TIME TO REFLECT

Elizabeth woke at dawn next morning and, for a moment, did not know why. Then from Lydia's room came the unmistakable sound of someone being very, very sick. She could tell the rest of the house was still asleep, so she slipped into her dressing gown and went next door.

Her youngest sister was on her knees over the chamber pot, weeping and retching, and Elizabeth's heart went out to her. She held Lydia's hair away from her face and, when she finally seemed to have finished, got a glass of water and a wet cloth to wipe her face. Lydia climbed back into bed and lay there, looking wretched. All at once, Elizabeth remembered the little girl who had followed Jane and her around, the child she had taught to tie her own shoelaces. She climbed onto the bed and took Lydia into her arms.

Lydia cried for a long time, not her usual, noisy, attention-seeking wail but a quiet, desperate weeping that was deeply affecting. Elizabeth held onto her sister, murmuring reassur-

ances, calling her "Lyddie-Lou" a name that had been indig-
nantly repudiated almost ten years ago.

"I didn't know!" said Lydia, eventually. "I didn't, Lizzy!"

"What didn't you know?"

"What he was going to do." She sniffed vigorously, and
Elizabeth went to get her a handkerchief. "I thought it was just
kissing, and he was so handsome, and he said he loved me."
She blew her nose noisily. "He hurt me, Lizzy. And now I've
got to go away on my own with no one to talk to where I don't
know anyone, and it's so unfair." The last few words sounded
rather more like the old Lydia, and Elizabeth was anxious not
to encourage her reappearance.

"You know there is no alternative, don't you?"

Lydia nodded reluctantly. "But I don't see why Kitty can't
come too. I won't have anyone to talk to, not even Maria
Lucas or Amelia Goulding or anyone."

"Because this might all still go wrong. People might still
find out, and then neither Maria nor Amelia nor anyone else
would ever be allowed to talk to you again." She hugged her
sister. "It will not last forever, and I promise to come and visit."

Lydia was silent for a few moments although she did not
move her head from its place on Elizabeth's shoulder. "Lizzy?"

"Yes?"

"Do you know anything about having a baby? No one will
tell me anything, and I'm so scared."

Elizabeth held on tighter. "I know very little, I'm afraid,
but you are going to stay with Aunt and Uncle Gardiner for a
few days before we go to Derbyshire. I am sure Aunt Gardiner
will be able to tell you anything you need to know. And if she
cannot, then write to me, and I promise to find out."

"Lizzy?"

"Yes, dear?"

"When it's time for the baby to come, will you or Jane
come and stay? I don't want it to be just Ma and me." This
was, Elizabeth reflected later, quite the most damning indict-
ment of her mother she had ever heard.

Lydia was still confined to her room, and when Elizabeth

looked in on her after breakfast, she saw her sister was still asleep. So she put on her bonnet and went for a walk, quite forgetting her promise to her mother not to stir from the house without an escort. "For there are deserters and I don't know who else hanging around, and we shall all be murdered in our beds, and Mrs Mason's strawberry beds quite stripped overnight."

Elizabeth always thought more clearly while walking, and she had a lot to consider.

It was not that she was displeased with the speed of events. It all made complete sense and promised a more satisfactory outcome for all concerned than she could possibly have imagined a few days earlier. It was just that she had barely had time to catch her breath. One moment, she had been cast into the depths of despair, and the next, she was engaged to be married to an excellent man who had promised to take care of everything, including herself.

She wondered, not for the first time, what Mr Darcy saw in her that had so captivated him. She had few illusions about her looks; she was by no means ill-favoured, but beside Jane, she knew she appeared positively plain. She was not even particularly accomplished; even if she practised regularly, something she usually avoided, she knew she was but an indifferent musician.

Perhaps, it was the way their minds seemed so well matched. She loved her father dearly, but she disagreed vehemently, if privately, with the way he conducted himself towards his family. Only with Mr Darcy had she met the combination of intelligence, education and... She struggled for the correct word, which was most unlike her. 'Devotion to duty' was almost correct but was too dry, too rigid, for the combination of generosity, insight, and industry she had come to admire.

She mounted the hill that faced towards Netherfield, looked out towards the house, and thought about her husband-to-be. Of course, he was a handsome man, his height matched by the breadth of his shoulders, and his looks were complemented by a very appealing gentleness that he extended not just to herself but to his sister and, so far as she had seen, to his servants, dependants, and friends.

She thought back to poor Lydia. Elizabeth, by dint of simply asking her Aunt Gardiner a few years ago, had a rather better idea of what the marriage bed entailed and did not believe that Mr Darcy (what *was* his first name?) would be careless of her or her person. She remembered the way they had kissed in the wood and felt again the curious frisson of excitement that merely thinking about it caused. She wondered whether there was a name for the curious pang of sensation below her navel that kissing him had given her. She giggled as she envisaged trying to ask someone, and then realised she could always ask him, though not, perhaps, just yet.

Netherfield seemed very close in the quiet of the early morning, and she considered walking over to visit him, but only briefly. However anxious she was to see him again, it would be most improper to call, uninvited and unannounced, and demand to see her intended husband, even if the expression on Caroline Bingley's face might make the journey worthwhile.

She did not want to return to Longbourn. It was too noisy, too chaotic. Her mother would still be in transports, and her father very probably hiding in his library. They would do better, she told herself firmly. She and Mr Darcy—she really must remember to ask him his first name—would be better parents and better friends than her own mother and father. She wondered about *his* parents and determined to ask him about them the next time they had a moment together, whenever that was.

She glanced at the sun and the shadows under the trees; it must be almost nine o'clock, and he had said he would call before luncheon. She turned to hurry home, suddenly anxious to see him again.

CHAPTER 17

DISCOVERIES AND EXPLANATIONS

"Fitzwilliam!"

As he entered the sitting room at Longbourn, she suddenly remembered the book-plate inside the Wordsworth he had given her all those months ago. The expression on his face in response to her greeting was almost shocking. Jane was present, so he could not and did not give full rein to his happiness; however, to someone who was watching him as closely as Elizabeth, the immediate shine in his eyes was as noticeable as that sudden smile at Rosings. For perhaps the first time, she realised the extent of her power over this man. To bring so much joy simply by using a man's Christian name!

Flustered, she took his hand and led him to the sofa. "I have been cudgelling my brains all morning, and only just now have I recalled your name. I fear I am a sad example of a bride-to-be."

He bent low, and she shivered as she felt the press of his lips, warm and dry, against the back of her hand. "There is much we shall have to learn about one another," he replied, and it seemed to her that his happiness was like a low hum in the room, warm and obscurely comforting. "I, for one, am looking forward to the process." Then suddenly anxious, he continued, "I hope you do not feel you are being rushed forward. If you would rather wait or make other arrangements than those we discussed yesterday with your father, I would be more than happy to accommodate your wishes."

She considered for a moment and thought that not the least of his good qualities was that he had both made the offer and was quite obviously not offended by her taking time to think it over. "No," she replied eventually. "I am not one of those women who long to spend months on preparations for their wedding. Now that the decision has been made, I find I am anxious to proceed." Then, catching sight of some lingering anxiety in his expressions, she added, "This is my own wish, quite apart from anything that needs to be done to deal with Lydia's situation."

This must have been on his mind, for his face cleared, and he turned to Jane. "I am afraid I bring Bingley's apologies, Miss Bennet. He remains at Netherfield to supervise Miss Bingley's departure. It has been decided that she is to stay with relatives in Scarborough for a time."

Jane, dear saintly Jane, actually looked concerned. "I do hope this has nothing to do with my marriage to her brother. I know she did not always look favourably upon it."

Elizabeth watched in fascination as her intended blushed deeply. "You need have no fear, Miss Bennet. It is not *your* marriage that has caused the rift." Jane looked confused and would doubtless have asked further if Elizabeth had not succeeded in frowning her into silence. "He hopes to visit this afternoon, after luncheon, if that would be agreeable. I have brought a groom to take a message if you have other engagements."

Regrettably, she did and had to leave the room to fetch pen and paper. Left alone together, Elizabeth and Mr Darcy fell silent. For the first time ever, Elizabeth found it difficult to look at him. He was so imposing—not just because he was tall, not just because he was well favoured, but because he was now and forever the most important person in her life, and really, what did she know about him? What did anybody ever know about the person they were about to marry? She remembered Charlotte Lucas once expressing the view that too much knowledge of one's spouse before marriage was a mistake. She had thought that was mistaken at the time; now she was doubly sure her friend was wrong. She wanted to know everything that could be known, and there was nothing to do but begin the voyage of discovery.

"Have you told your sister?" she asked.

This time a smile did break. "I did indeed. She is delighted for both of us and hopes that you and Miss Bennet will not forget that you both undertook to come to Netherfield tomorrow afternoon." He had the grace to look a little shame-faced. "She wanted to come with me this morning, but I am afraid I did not wish to share you."

There she could and did scold him gently, finding it easier and easier to talk once she had begun. "Georgiana and I must get to know each other better, and we cannot do so if you keep me to yourself. I am in some ways marrying her as well as you, and another sister is not an undertaking to be made lightly."

He laid a large hand over hers. "I am so glad you feel as you do. Georgiana has been far too isolated, especially since our father died, and you are almost as much a godsend to her as you are for me."

Jane came back in just as Elizabeth was considering laying her other hand upon his. The warmth of his skin was so very noticeable and, yes, comforting. They had to part so that the message could be sent, and then it was decided that all three of them and Kitty would walk in the woods. Jane walked with Kitty and was discreet without in any way emulating their mother's impropriety, engaging Kitty in conversation and allowing Elizabeth and Mr Darcy to talk.

It was a happy inspiration that caused her to enquire about Pemberley, the discussion of which brought out all the energy, enthusiasm, and eloquence she had come to admire. "I think it quite the most beautiful place on earth," he said. "Even now after the damage caused to the gardens by the recent floods, it is a place of peace and growing things. I particularly look forward to showing you the park. There are woods and streams, glades of bluebells and clearings full of daffodils in the spring. And beyond the park, there are the peaks—moors, cliffs, and rocks for you to see and explore. It is rather colder than you are accustomed to here in Hertfordshire, the country-side less regulated and controlled, but it has its own, particular beauty that I hope you will come to love as much as I do."

There was much food for thought in this description, not least his recognition of the importance to her of the outdoor life. Her mother had always declared that no husband would ever allow his wife to go gallivanting round the countryside. In this, as in so much else, her mother had been proved wrong.

His description of the house, though just as proud, was rather more daunting. Without showing away in any fashion, he could not help informing her of its sheer size. She had been imagining something similar to a slightly grander Netherfield, not a house with a library that extended over two floors, a long gallery, and a ballroom. She wondered whether she could enquire after the number of bedrooms without sounding vulgar or acquisitive, and then decided not to. No matter its size, Mr Darcy believed her capable of becoming its mistress, and even if she were not now, she could no doubt learn.

Amidst happier topics, they could not avoid a discussion of Lydia. She and their mother were to leave that very afternoon in Mr Darcy's coach, and the news of their visit to Mr and Mrs Gardiner was to be given to the neighbourhood after church on Sunday. The engagement of Mr Darcy to Elizabeth was to be announced at the same time in the hope that it would provide a more fertile ground for conversation and spec-ulation. Neither Elizabeth nor Mr Darcy was happy about this use of their engagement, nor at willingly inviting the specula-tion and tattle of their neighbours although both were resigned to its necessity.

As they strolled along the well-worn paths, Elizabeth tucked her hand into his arm, and he placed his hand over hers. After a few minutes, he was stroking the back with his thumb, a tiny movement Elizabeth found curiously unsettling: not unpleasant—certainly not unpleasant—merely disturbing. How could such a small gesture affect her so profoundly? She caught him once, glancing down at their joined hands, and knew that he, too, felt something of this. Warmth seemed to spread outwards from her hand to her arm and then to the rest of her person, and once again, that strange pang of feeling. She leaned her head on his arm, and he sighed with satisfaction.

She was acutely conscious that they were not alone and that she dearly wished they were. She wanted him to kiss her again, and she wanted to know again the sensation of absolute security that his arms had come to represent. But they were not alone, and they were not married, and for the first time, the estate of 'married woman' seemed infinitely desirable.

At last, as they re-entered Longbourn, Jane came to her rescue. Without in any way seeming to do so on purpose, she managed their arrival so that she and Kitty went indoors first, leaving Elizabeth and Mr Darcy alone to enter the drawing room. She could not ask, but she could look. He saw and, in two strides, was before her. With infinite gentleness, he cradled her head in his fingers and bent his head to hers. She could feel one little finger rubbing softly behind her ear as their lips met, and it was just as wonderful as the first time. No—more wonderful because she knew to open her mouth to his tongue and to touch it with her own; knew for the first time the joy of hearing him groan, a rumbling noise deep in his chest. Whatever was happening to her, it was happening to both of them.

There was the sound of voices in the hallway, and they parted reluctantly. It was fortunate for them that it was Mrs Bennet who entered with Jane, for anyone with more perception would surely have noticed their dazed silence.

Church next day was every bit the ordeal Elizabeth had feared. The buzz of speculation started the moment Mr Darcy and Mr Bingley arrived and joined them in the family pew. When Elizabeth and Mr Darcy shared her prayer-book, it increased perceptibly, despite the frowns of the parson. Her only consolation was that, in sharing prayer and hymn books, their hands often touched, which was most enjoyable but hardly conducive to due attention to one's religious duties. There was also something strangely satisfying in singing together, and it seemed to her that her mezzo and his baritone were the only two voices to be heard. However, careful consultation with Jane afterwards revealed that this had not actually been the case.

As they left, the gossips descended, disguising their rapacity for news in enquiring after Mrs Bennet and Lydia. Any interest in them disappeared the moment Mr Bennet advised Mrs Philips to watch for wedding announcements in the *Times*, and Elizabeth could almost see her intended brace himself for the onslaught of good wishes and, more or less, genteel enquiry. She did her best to shelter him from the worst of the curiosity and was gratified to see his shoulders loosen and his face take on a less forbidding mien. She heard him mutter something to himself occasionally, especially after a particularly effusive address, and she was greatly amused when she learned of the Darcy family's new motto: 'reserved but polite.' Perhaps she could have some book-plates made; it would be their first private joke. When they finally escaped, it was with promises that they would all meet at Netherfield after luncheon.

CHAPTER 18

AN UNDESIRABLE VISITOR

IT WAS A BEAUTIFUL AFTERNOON AS ELIZABETH AND JANE RODE to Netherfield in Mr Darcy's carriage. It was almost too hot, and the clouds were high and wispy in the brilliant blue sky. Mr Bennet had refused to let Mary and Kitty come along, insisting that they spend their time in some rational and, in Mary's case, non-Fordycian manner.

Mrs Hurst was waiting to greet them, and it quickly became apparent that she was determined to be gracious and welcoming. Whether this was due to her own goodwill or fear of her suddenly decisive brother, Elizabeth was unable to determine.

Georgiana was everything that was loving, hurrying to embrace her future sister, words tumbling over themselves as she hastened to assure Elizabeth of her own happiness and her assurance of her brother's future felicity. Elizabeth very quickly saw traces of the young woman Georgiana could be with her own help and encouragement. As she looked past Georgiana, she could see Mr Darcy looking at them both fondly, and recognised that her own hopes for their marriage stood on firm foundations.

The afternoon was full of surprises, not the least of which was Mr Hurst's shy production of his flute. Every one of them with any pretence at skill had their turn, although it was quickly obvious that the Darcys, brother and sister, were the true musicians amongst them. There was very little sheet music for their ill-assorted selection of instruments, but they managed to enjoy themselves and entertain their listeners. Elizabeth, in particular, found that she loved to watch Mr Darcy play. His eyes rarely left hers, and it seemed to her that he played directly to and for her. She remembered the evening at Rosings when she had so misjudged his actions and realised that he had been playing for her then too. She smiled; his face seemed to light up, and his fingers to dance on the strings.

After the music, they adjourned to the sitting room for tea and cakes. No one knew why Mr Darcy insisted on providing Elizabeth with a footstool she did not need in the slightest, and Jane resolved to discover why this made Elizabeth blush. The conversation was much livelier than any Elizabeth had known at Netherfield, and she spared half a second to feel sorry for Miss Bingley, who was missing so much through nobody's fault but her own.

When tea had finished, Mrs Hurst and Mr Bingley invited Jane to look over her future home, Mr Hurst wandered off somewhere, and Elizabeth, Mr Darcy, and Georgiana stayed behind to talk.

"Sir," said Elizabeth sternly. "You may find something to occupy yourself while your sister and I become better acquainted."

Georgiana looked rather alarmed at this mode of address, but Mr Darcy merely smiled and bowed. "Yes ma'am," he replied. "I shall retire to the desk. Georgie, I am writing to our uncle. Let me know if there is anything you wish me to include."

"Now then, Miss Darcy," said Elizabeth, "let us have a

cosy chat. It is not every day one meets a new sister."

Georgiana blushed and had to be coaxed into conversation, the first flush of enthusiasm at the door to Netherfield having exhausted her courage. However, after a few minutes, they were 'Georgie' and 'Lizzy,' and after a very few minutes more, she felt comfortable enough to produce her needlework, some handkerchiefs she was embroidering for her brother and for Elizabeth. It did not take long for Elizabeth to confirm her first impressions of a young lady of sense and education who lacked only a little confidence to be a welcome addition to any circle. Without being immodest, Elizabeth knew she could be of great assistance to her new sister and was glad that there was something else she could bring to the marriage, other than whatever it was that Mr Darcy saw in her.

They had not been talking long when Georgiana rummaged around in her workbox and pronounced herself out of a particular colour of thread. "But it is no matter, for I have more in my room upstairs." And with that, she left the room.

Elizabeth and Mr Darcy looked at one another and smiled. "I suspect that is my sister's idea of romantic discretion," he said. "I shall have to ask Mrs Annesley to have a word with her when she gets back from visiting her brother."

"She is a lovely girl."

"I know, and I am delighted to see you becoming friends. You are both very dear to me, and I would be distressed if she felt herself neglected in any way."

They looked at one another across the room. The curtains at the open windows billowed in the slight breeze, and the only sounds were birdsong and footsteps overhead as the inspection party passed from room to room.

"We cannot," they both said together and laughed.

"They might be back at any moment," he said, "and we have to set Georgie a good example."

Elizabeth could not help but laugh. "Oh dear, I am not sure I like being a good example. Can I not be an awful warning instead?"

He got up and strode over to her, and she was never afterwards sure whether he had intended to move. He took her hands in his and kissed them both, one after the other, and then led her over to a high-backed chair.

"Now, madam, you can sit where I cannot see you and drink your tea while I finish writing my letters without distraction." He brought the footstool before the chair, and she rested her slippers upon it. "There—you can think of what might have been instead of tormenting me." She smiled up at him from beneath her lashes, and he had to tear himself away.

Back at the writing desk, he pulled the paper towards him and continued his letter to his uncle Matlock. He wondered briefly how the news would be received and then shrugged. He owed no duty to anyone but himself and Elizabeth and, while he hoped that his uncle would be happy for him, had no intention whatsoever of being swayed by any disapproval.

After his uncle, he penned a brief note to Lady Catherine. He owed his mother's sister that much at least, although he had no hope of anything but ill manners in reply. He saw a slim arm and hand reach out, replace the empty cup and saucer, and take up one of the books he had left on a side table. He wondered how she would enjoy *Marmion* as he took up another sheet of paper, determined to write to his great-uncle, Sir James Darcy. His father had been estranged from the older man, and Darcy had followed his father's lead. He was no longer sure that this was always wise, and he paused a moment to think best how to word the letter.

"Got you, you bastard!" Framed in the open window, pistol in hand, was a familiar if ragged figure.

"Wickham!"

"Sit down and shut up, Darcy. This is loaded, and I've nothing to lose." He flung a long leg over the windowsill and climbed in.

He doesn't know Elizabeth is in the room. Oh God, if he finds out, then there is no telling which of us he might shoot. And Georgie might come back at any moment.

"What do you want, Wickham?" The bell pull was at the other end of the fireplace, well away from either of them. There was no way to summon help.

"I want you to suffer, you bastard. You've got everything, and you've made damn sure I got nothing! Nothing!" Wickham was shouting now, almost in tears, and he was standing not far from the high-backed chair in which *she* was sitting.

"If it is money you want—"

"I want what is rightfully mine. I want Pemberley."

Dear God, the man is mad. Wickham looked thin and feverish, the hand that held the pistol grimy and unsteady.

"Killing me will get you nothing but a noose."

"Be worth it to see you done down. I should have been heir. I was the one he loved, not you—boring, rigid, dull, dull, dull."

"Is that what you've thought all these years?" Darcy pushed back his chair and stood, not caring that the pistol came up and pointed at his heart, desperate to make Wickham shoot before he could choose another target. "Don't you understand? I am the son he made in his own image. You were merely entertainment."

"NO!"

The cocking of the pistol was audible in the room, and Darcy put one hand on the desk, preparing to vault it in an effort to get to Wickham if the shot missed or misfired. Before he could do so, something came flying round the back of Elizabeth's chair, grasped in a slender hand, and caught Wickham squarely on the back of the head. He crashed face down on the floor. The pistol discharged with a crack like lightning as the room filled with smoke.

Darcy rushed round to him, kicking the pistol aside and running his hands over Wickham's prone body, looking for other weapons. A long knife he found thrust into the back of the belt under the coat was tossed out of the window. The room filled with people: Bingley, Hurst, two burly-looking footmen. Wickham was seized, blood pouring from his broken nose. He looked stunned and bewildered. The footstool that had hit him was kicked under a sofa, and he was led away, struggling feebly, to be locked in a cellar.

At last, it was safe for Darcy to take Elizabeth in his arms. She was trembling—as well she might—and he could tell that tears were not far away, so he rocked her gently, calling her his brave love, his valiant Elizabeth, until she raised her head. "I could not let him," she said. "I was sitting in that chair, and I knew I could not let him." Then firmly and loud enough for everyone to hear, she said, "You are mine! I will not let anyone hurt you!"

He kissed her then, in front of Bingley, the Hursts, his sister, and hers. Had they been alone, he would have carried her off and made her his. She twined her arms round his neck, neither of them caring that he had lifted her off her feet. He kissed her eyes, her cheeks, her throat. She shivered and hung on to him, her knuckles white where they grasped his lapels.

A loud cough from Bingley brought them, blushing, to their senses. He set her back on her feet and had to watch as Jane and Georgiana descended on her with cries of alarm and concern.

Bingley took his arm and led him into a corner. "Shall I send for the constable?"

Darcy shook his head. "No, I cannot do that to him."

"He tried to kill you, man!"

"We grew up together. I cannot hang the man I went fishing with when we were both boys." He shook his head. "The ironic thing is, he might have been a brother to me if he had not hated me. Yet he loved my father who treated him like a lapdog."

"You mean to let him go free?" Bingley was looking at him as though he were mad.

"No. I shall have him shipped off to the Americas or somewhere. Perhaps he can make something of himself over there." He smiled wryly. "It is fortunate I have no plans to visit the colonies. I suspect I would arrive there to find myself painted as the blackest ⬛ from hell." He clapped Bingley on the shoulder. "If you don't mind keeping him locked up overnight, I shall take him up to the Pool of London in the morning and send him off."

"With a present of money and a suitable outfit, knowing you," said Bingley, but he did not attempt to dissuade his friend, who went back to sit with Elizabeth.

Jane took Georgiana by the arm and led her to a different sofa, and Darcy and his Elizabeth sat together, hand in hand, her head resting on his shoulder until it was time for her to go home.

Darcy rode back to Longbourn in the coach with Jane and Elizabeth, and while Jane perseveringly looked out of the window, he sat opposite and held Elizabeth's hands in his.

"Sweetheart," he said as they left the grounds of Netherfield Park. "If it meets with your approval, I would rather ship Wickham overseas than hand him over to the constable. I shall do my best to ensure he never returns to this country." He sighed. "We were boys together, and I am sadly convinced that many of his faults may be attributed to the way my father dealt with him."

"Surely, he must bear the lion's share of the responsibility for his own actions."

"Perhaps, but my father made much of him, enjoyed his conversation and easy manner. Wickham was the son of my father's steward, a worthy and respectable man. But my father, in paying for his education and keeping him so much about him, gave him expectations that were not and could not be met. I never before realised Wickham thought my father preferred him to me. What he did not realise was that the rigours of my own education and upbringing were what my father considered necessary for his heir. Wickham was allowed to be idle and charming only because, in the end, he was unimportant. I cannot but think that cruel of my father."

Elizabeth pondered for a moment, trying to bring her mind to bear on the problem of Wickham's fate. However, her thoughts slipped into contemplation of her lover's generosity and from there, by easy stages, into the way his hair curled, the fact that it was not black, as she had first decided, but merely dark brown with occasional lighter tones and shades.

She shook herself back into attention. "I own I have no desire to see any man hang," she said, "but neither do I wish your life to be in danger in the future. If you can be sure he will not return, then I agree."

He leaned forward and kissed her hands, so she seized her opportunity to touch his hair, feeling the curls spring against her palms. He raised his head and there was something in his eyes so fierce and yet so tender, she could hardly bring herself to meet his gaze.

"I shall take him up to London tomorrow."

"You will not go alone, surely?"

"No, no, I promise. However, I am afraid I shall have to be away for several days. I must make plans for Miss Lydia's reception in Derbyshire, and there is much that needs to be set in train for our wedding. I shall speak to your father today to make arrangements, but I think we should begin the preparations for moving to London and then on to Pemberley. If you are in agreement, that is."

She tightened her grip on his fingers. "I do not wish to wait a single second longer than is absolutely necessary," she said firmly, and was rewarded by the brilliant smile she had first seen at Rosings all those months ago.

Following the discussion with Mr Bennet, it was decided that the family would remove to Darcy House the following Saturday, Mrs Bennet and Lydia to remain with Mr and Mrs Gardiner. Elizabeth woke early next morning and stationed herself in the window of her mother's room overlooking the road; she was gratified by the sight of Mr Darcy's coach with two stout footmen on the box and her lover's face in the window, looking for her to exchange waved greetings.

CHAPTER 19

MATTERS TO SETTLE

Elizabeth was in such a ferment to be away that she had packed her few belongings by the end of Monday afternoon and was reduced to mooning around the house until her father packed her off outdoors for a long walk, safe in the knowledge that the source of the recent depredations was being hustled out of the country. While she was out, Mr Bingley called, and it was confirmed that she and Jane were to share a wedding in the church at Lambton, the village where Mrs Gardiner had spent much of her childhood.

By Tuesday afternoon, Jane had packed the clothes she wished to take, and the two sisters were further reduced to discussing the manifold excellencies of their respective betrotheds. Elizabeth was forced to concede that she now knew the state of her affections with some degree of precision. Any inclination that Jane may have felt to tease her sister was effectively stifled when Elizabeth suggested discussing tongues with Mr Bingley the next time Jane had the opportunity to kiss him.

On Wednesday, a letter arrived for Mr Bennet from Mr Darcy with an enclosure for Elizabeth. She seized it and ran to her chamber to peruse it in peace and privacy.

Darcy House, Grosvenor Square
London

My Dear Elizabeth,
It seems strangely unfair that my first letter to you, my darling, should be full of mundane business, but I feel I should inform you that I am just come from the docks where I have arranged passage for Wickham to India. I have left him in no doubt that a return to England means his death, and I have correspondents in that country to whom I can entrust watch over him. The broken nose you gave him should go far to hamper his efforts to ingratiate himself with the fairer sex.

There, that is out of the way, and I can enquire of my beloved how she does. I devoutly trust you suffer no ill effects from the shocking events on Sunday. I miss you quite dreadfully despite having seen you so very few days ago. My only consolation is that the work I do now will help establish our new life on the firmest of footings.

I have written to Bridger and his wife to prepare the cottage for Miss Lydia and to Nurse Grayson to secure her aid. I have set Darcy House on its ears preparing for your arrival. My parents' chambers, which have been empty for many years, are being opened and cleaned. I have not ventured on any decorative changes since I feel sure you will have your own tastes and fancies, and I wish that you should make this house as much your home as Longbourn has been.

I hope you will not feel I am being indelicate when I say how much I look forward to seeing you in this familiar setting. The kiss we shared in the drawing room at Netherfield is much on my mind, and I have, as promised, ordered a selection of footstools to be distributed about the house. I wish we were married already, sharing this house and our lives. I dream about you, and where once my dreams were confused and distressing, now I awake calm and contented, relieved that another day is passing and I am another day closer to seeing you again.

Never to spend another day apart is the devout wish of your most humble and loving—
Fitzwilliam Darcy

If this were not enough to disturb her equilibrium, the discussion of her marriage settlement, details of which Mr Darcy had sent to Mr Bennet, certainly was. She had always known him to be wealthy; however, the sheer extent of that wealth was a shock. The amount that Mr Darcy had determined to settle upon her by way of income and of provision in case he predeceased her, seemed, to her at least, ridiculously generous.

She was somewhat distressed and, although she resolved not to let him know, was relieved when he arrived on the Thursday, alerted by some passing comment in the letter from Mr Bennet agreeing to the terms. They walked in the garden since her sisters were all out at their aunt Philips's, doing their best to stem the tide of gossip and speculation arising from the recent flood of incident.

Elizabeth could not take his arm as she tried to express something of her misgivings and was charmed all over again by his grave attention to her concerns. "There are two aspects of this matter I would like you to consider," he said when she had finished. "Firstly, I am a man of considerable means, and I dearly wish you, as my wife, to share in those means. Although I sincerely hope to spend many years with you, in the event that I cannot, I shall not leave you dependent upon anyone's goodwill." He took her hand and threaded it through his arm. "Secondly, my dear, in the circles in which we shall move, any want of attention on my part will be seen as a reflection of my regard for you. I love you, and I do not wish anyone to be in any doubt of that."

"But, Fitzwilliam, I bring so little to——"

"Elizabeth, you have brought me everything! Can you not see? I had almost succeeded in turning myself into my father, a man without connexion to the world save as patron, landlord, or master. I was becoming mired in my own pride and conceit until I met you. I had even begun to neglect my poor sister." He sighed and shook his head. "Even were we to part today, I should be the better man for having known you, and since we are not to part, I do not believe there is anything we cannot accomplish together, you and I."

She stopped and looked up at him. "You give me too much credit. You are a good man, Fitzwilliam. You always were."

"I am a better and a far happier man now." He fumbled in his pocket and produced a small box. "There are bigger, more opulent jewels waiting for you at home, but you have such small hands, I thought you would prefer this." The ring was beautiful, a single diamond on a simple, gold band. "It was my grandmother's," he said as he slipped it on her finger. "I hope you will wear it and remember how very much I love you and long to make you my wife."

She lifted her face, and he bent low to kiss her. Then she threaded her arms round his waist, beneath his coat, and rested her head on his chest, feeling his warmth and the steady beat of his heart. "I still think you overestimate my worth," she said. "For it seems I suffer from a sad lack of resolution..."

He rested his cheek on her head, and they stood until the sound of voices in the road revealed that Jane, Mary, and Kitty had returned.

CHAPTER 20

LONDON

THE JOURNEY TO LONDON WAS QUITE THE EASIEST THE BENNET family had ever undertaken. A modern, well-sprung carriage, excellent horses, and frequent stops for rest and refreshment gave Elizabeth her first real experience of the luxury her new life would afford. Even Kitty was somewhat silenced, not least by the way Mr Darcy's servants referred to her as 'Miss Catherine' and offered cordials for her cough.

It seemed to take much longer to reach Grosvenor Square than it ever had to reach Gracechurch Street, and the house, when they finally arrived was quite the largest any of them had entered in London. Mr Darcy and his sister were waiting to greet them, and their warmth went some way towards easing the Bennet sisters' embarrassment.

For the first time in their lives, the Bennet sisters had not only a room to themselves but also a maid. Elizabeth and Jane were separated only by a connecting door and were soon in and out of each other's room, exchanging impressions. Georgiana arrived and was quickly included as all four sisters gathered in Elizabeth's room to talk.

"Of course," said Georgiana, "this is only a guest room. The mistress's room is upstairs. Fillum says I should take you up and show you round later."

"Fillum?"

Georgiana blushed. "I could not pronounce his name when I was very small, so I called him Fillum. Sometimes, the name still slips out."

Amidst much laughter, Georgiana was introduced to 'Ane,' 'Izbit,' 'Airy,' and 'Taffrin.' As they came downstairs for tea, still giggling together, Elizabeth found Darcy waiting in the hall, an expression of bemused happiness on his face. He took her arm and led her into the drawing room. "I had not realised just how quiet and dull this house had become until I heard you all laughing."

"I fear you must become accustomed to it, sir," replied Elizabeth. "For I dearly love to laugh."

With a look half-embarrassed, half-proud, Georgiana served them all tea. All except Mr Bennet who had left to visit his wife and Lydia and was not expected to return before dinner. Elizabeth had been greatly reassured by her first glimpses of Darcy House; while beautifully appointed, it had none of the ostentation or useless finery of Rosings.

After tea, Mr Darcy pleaded business and retired to his study with his London secretary, a thin, bespectacled young man who met him in the hall with a pile of correspondence and a despondent expression. As she led them up the stairs on a tour of the house, Georgiana giggled. "Poor Mr Handley. He thinks my brother ought to make his mark in politics. I do not think he has ever been reconciled to Fitzwilliam's hatred of the mere idea."

There was a lot to see, and gradually first Mary then Kitty and, at last, Jane dropped out of the tour, Jane to write to Mr Bingley who had also returned to London. Elizabeth, however, was fascinated and willingly followed her new sister along corridors and into rooms. The library was especially impressive, and the formal dining room was, to her dazzled eyes, quite the most handsome room she had ever seen. Upstairs, there was a collection of formal portraits, and for the first time, she saw likenesses of Mr Darcy's parents.

"There are better paintings at Pemberley," said Georgiana airily, and would have passed them, but Elizabeth stopped to take a better look. Mr Darcy's mother had been a remarkably handsome woman with a distinct resemblance to her son, especially about the eyes and nose, although she had been fair where he was dark. Mr Darcy senior was obviously the source of his colouring and height, judging by the horse that stood behind him. The expression on his father's face recalled Fitzwilliam at his most proud.

"I did not know my mother," said Georgiana suddenly. "She died when I was very small."

"She was very lovely." Elizabeth turned to look at her. "You have her eyes."

Georgiana contemplated the picture for a moment, her head to one side. "They were not happy," she said dispassionately. "Everyone says so. The marriage was arranged between their parents and…" She shrugged. "According to my aunt Matlock, they hardly ever lived together. She stayed here in London, and my father stayed at Pemberley."

"And your brother?"

"Oh, he stayed at Pemberley; he was so very ill all the time."

This was quite unexpected. Elizabeth thought back to the height and broad shoulders of her intended and had to ask. "Ill? In what way?"

"According to Mrs Reynolds, the housekeeper at Pemberley, he had a terrible cough. They say you could hear the wheezing all over the house. Everyone thought he was consumptive. Then one day, just after I was born, it stopped, and he started growing." Then she added quite matter-of-factly, "I think I was only born because they thought Fitzwilliam was going to die, and my father wanted an heir."

Elizabeth drew her shawl around her. While she knew that

it was her duty to provide her husband with children, the idea that they might be provided first and foremost to service her husband's property struck her as deeply unnatural, and she was silent as Georgiana led her through the rest of the rooms. Even the mistress's apartments, for they could scarcely be called rooms, called forth little comment. She wandered through the bedroom, the dressing room, the bathing room, and even the sitting room and while she could see that they were warm and well-furnished, and could be easily transformed into something more to her own taste, she could give no more than abstracted replies to Georgiana's enquiries and barely noticed when she left.

Elizabeth sat down on the great four-poster bed and wondered whether what she was feeling was mere nerves. Surely, every man desired an heir to his estate. Did possessing a great estate make that need more pressing? Suppose she failed? Suppose she produced only daughters? She thought of two people who did not love or perhaps even like each other feeling obliged to... She did not know the words for what husband and wife did together, even if she knew what they did.

"Elizabeth? Is something wrong?"

Hearing Darcy's voice, relief flooded through her for a moment before she realised that, in this instance, he was the source of at least some of her disquiet.

"Georgiana came to find me. She fears she has said something to upset you."

This, at least, she could dispel. "No, no, it was nothing she said. It is merely that I have come to realise the responsibility I have assumed."

"It is only a house, my dear. A little larger than you are used to but——"

"No, that is not what I mean." He sat down beside her on the bed, and the impropriety did not even occur to her. "I love you dearly, Fitzwilliam." He kissed the hand he held. "But I am my mother's daughter—one of five! What if I cannot bear you sons?"

"Then we shall leave everything to our daughters or Georgiana's children if we have none at all. We can none of us see the future, my love, but if mine holds only you—then I am more than satisfied." He took her chin in gentle fingers and turned her face to his. "Pemberley is not entailed, and even if it were, I tried to live my life solely in its service and was miserable." He kissed her gently on the forehead. "I would far rather have you and be happy."

Elizabeth attempted to dry her eyes with her fingers and accepted his handkerchief as a substitute. "It is most provoking when you have rational answers to all my fears."

He stood up and drew her to her feet. "Come, we cannot be found here. There will be talk."

He continued speaking as they left the room and headed downstairs. "You surely do not think I am without my own fears? What do I know of how to be a husband? My father was no basis for emulation, and my mother visited but rarely, appearing as some glittering dream of silk and jewels and then disappearing again. You were born to be happy. I worry that I might not make you so."

She let him descend a few steps before her, and when he turned to see why she did not follow, she looked round, saw they were alone, and kissed him swiftly on the lips. "If you continue as you have begun, my…my love"—*why was that so difficult to say?* she wondered—"then I have no fears on that score." He would have kissed her back, but she scampered past him down the stairs to where a greatly relieved Georgiana was waiting for them.

CHAPTER 21

A FATHER'S PREROGATIVE

WHEN ELIZABETH AND JANE CAME DOWN FOR DINNER THAT evening, they found their father waiting but no sign of Kitty and Mary—let alone Mrs Bennet, whom they had expected to come to dine. "I visited your mother and Lydia this afternoon," he said. "And I am most seriously displeased." He had a glass of what looked like brandy in his hand and drank from it copiously. "From what your Aunt Gardiner informs me, it is perfectly obvious that your mother has done little or nothing to prepare her daughters for adult life. Lydia appears to have learnt nothing from her situation and is both impenitent and absurd in her demands. I have told your mother that she is not to call here unless I tell her she may. Moreover, Mary and Kitty are no longer to be considered 'out' until I am convinced they are ready. I shall be hiring a governess for them both—or at least a lady who can give them the guidance their mother has signally failed to provide."

Elizabeth thought about protesting this one-sided allocation of responsibility but decided it was a conversation best left for when they could be assured of privacy. She contented herself with asking after Mary and Kitty.

"Since they are no longer out," said her father, "and since Lord Matlock is coming to dine, they will take their dinner upstairs. I understand Miss Darcy is to keep them company."

This was news to fluster the steadiest of nerves. Although Mr Darcy was indubitably his own master, the Earl of Matlock was his nearest and oldest male relative and perhaps the nearest to a father he had living. Elizabeth had done her best, but she had been forced to don a gown that had already seen much wear, her only jewels: her garnet cross and the ring Mr Darcy had given her.

As Mr Darcy and his uncle came into the room together, she saw a heavy-set man of medium height with his sister's fair colouring but not her looks. He appeared dour, almost sullen, and there was no sign of the charm and good humour of his son Colonel Fitzwilliam.

Darcy watched as Elizabeth, who had found herself sitting opposite the earl for dinner, did her best to engage him in conversation. He could tell the exact moment she realised his uncle was not ill humoured, merely shy and ill at ease.

After a few civil commonplaces, Elizabeth had ventured a question about her betrothed's childhood and had tempted the earl into a series of reminiscences which revealed both his kindness and his pride in his nephew. "Gave him his first pony when he was six," he said, entirely forgetting his turbot in his enthusiasm. "Bravest lad on a horse I ever saw. Not a hard-goer or heavy handed, mind, got a real feel for the animal. He and my youngest boy, he's a colonel in the dragoons now, y' know, were following the hunt when most lads their age are still on leading reins." Darcy sat back, content to see his uncle display all the most generous aspects of his character under Elizabeth's gentle questioning.

Georgiana came down for dessert to see her uncle, and he

could also see that Mr Bennet was relieved when Lord Matlock greeted her affectionately.

The ladies and gentlemen did not separate after dinner, but the earl quite obviously wanted to talk to him, so Darcy took him into the library for a glass of port and a cigar. "Your aunt Catherine has been writing," said Lord Matlock bluntly. "Lot of nonsense. Take no notice of her. I shan't."

"I don't."

"Good." Matlock stared round the room as though searching for inspiration, but Darcy knew he was only gathering his thoughts. "Look, my boy," he said eventually. "We both know I'm not a clever fellow. Your mother got all the brains in the family. But I can see your Miss Elizabeth is a nice girl, and I can see she makes you happy. She's good to Georgie too, and we both know there are many who would not be. And she thinks the world of you. Your aunt Augusta has been talking a lot of nonsense. Well, I will not have it. Could see you were low at Christmas and before then, and… well, any young lady who can put a stop to that is good enough for me. Bring her over to Alfreton when you're ready, and I shall make sure she's welcome." He patted Darcy clumsily on the arm. "Congratulations, my boy. You've found yourself a good 'un."

Darcy was deeply touched as he wrung his uncle's hand. He would have to discuss it with Elizabeth, but next Christmas he wanted to invite his uncle, aunt, and cousins to Pemberley. No more dull, uncomfortable evenings—she would show them all a holiday, not just of peace and plenty but of joy and good humour. He knew she had her fears, but he also knew she would be the making of him and his family.

He took his uncle back into the drawing room where they drank coffee and listened to Georgiana and Elizabeth play. She was wearing the lavender-coloured gown and his ring. Soon he would give her diamonds, but she would look no more beautiful that she did now.

His uncle left soon afterwards, Jane went to read a letter from Bingley, Mr Bennet wandered off to the library—

although not before giving his daughter and future son a stern, admonitory look—and they were alone.

"I cannot stay long," she said.

"I know." They were sitting side by side on the sofa, and just for a moment, they held hands. "My uncle approves. It would have made no difference, but I thought you would like to know."

"I am glad." Then in a sudden rush. "Fitzwilliam, when can we be married?"

He kissed her, running his fingers lightly along the line of her jaw, sending ripples of sensation over her skin and deep into her bones. "If there were only the two of us to consider, I would say tomorrow," he replied a little breathlessly. "However, I assume you would wish to purchase your wedding clothes..." He kissed her through her attempt at protest. "And I also assume you would like your mother, Lydia, and the Gardiners to attend..." He waited, but this time there was no protest, so he continued. "I have sent word to Pemberley to start preparing rooms for everyone. I have the licence, and the church at Lambton should soon stand ready. My uncle is to go to Derbyshire to ready my aunt and cousins..."

He kissed her again, shivering as she, greatly daring, ran her fingers through his hair. "Do that again, madam," he growled, "and it will be tomorrow, if not tonight!"

She giggled happily and did it again.

He took himself off to the end of the sofa just as Mr Bennet came in from the library, seeming somewhat surprised at the distance between them. "We were just discussing the date for our wedding, sir," said Darcy, attempting to carry off his discomposure with aplomb. "Did you ask your brother Gardiner when he could travel?"

"What? Oh yes. Tell me, my boy, where did you get this volume of Aeschylus?"

Darcy took the book, examined it, and returned it. "My grandfather bought it in Paris before the war. What did Mr Gardiner say?"

"Paris? Hmmm…" He was about to wander off again when his daughter seized his arm.

"Don't be such a tease, Papa. When did Uncle Gardiner say he could travel to Derbyshire with us?"

"Oh yes. Next week, any day after Wednesday?"

Elizabeth held out her hand. Darcy took it and kissed it. "Would you care to be married next Saturday, my love?" he said.

"Sir, I believe I should like it above all things."

CHAPTER 22

DRAMA AND DEVOTION

To Elizabeth's considerable surprise, the appearance of the Bennet family in the Darcy family pew caused almost as much of a sensation as Mr Darcy's had in the church at Longbourn. She was perfectly certain that unfriendly eyes were assessing her looks, her gown, and her probable worth and might have been made uneasy had she not recalled with some satisfaction that the only person whose good opinion she was obliged to court was sitting next to her, sharing her hymn book.

Outside the church, more than one interested party came forward in the hope of valuable information, only to retire unsatisfied in the face of Mr Darcy's imperturbable hauteur and Elizabeth's good-humoured refusal to be awed, condescended to, or discomposed.

After luncheon, it was decided that Elizabeth and Jane would visit Gracechurch Street. Even Mr Bennet conceded that it would be too cruel to exclude their mother from any discussion of their bridal finery. With only a few days in which to purchase and order everything needed, they would have to be very busy indeed.

The two sisters made their way across London in an entirely different carriage from the one in which they had travelled from Hertfordshire, two footmen behind and a maid inside the coach with them, which effectively prevented them from discussing everything they most desired to discuss now that they were alone for the first time in days. Elizabeth dearly wished for Jane's reassurance of her ability to manage her new position while Jane was just as eager for Elizabeth's reassurance of Mr Bingley's regard, given that he had been out of London on business for the last week.

The house at Gracechurch Street was much quieter than either of them had expected in view of the presence of their mother and Lydia. At first, Elizabeth was inclined to attribute this to the usual calm good sense of their aunt and uncle; however, it quickly became apparent that this was not the case.

Mrs Bennet and Lydia had been accommodated in a large room to the rear of the house that was doing service as a bedroom and sitting room combined. Lydia was lying down when they arrived, and Jane went over to sit on the bed while Elizabeth joined their mother on the sofa.

She heard Jane say, "Are you quite well, Lydia?"

And Lydia's reply: "Oh, Jane, I'm so glad you're here. I do feel queer," before her attention was claimed by her mother, who was pale and had obviously not slept well. For the first time she could remember, Elizabeth thought her mother might be ill in truth.

"Lizzy, Jane. So your father has allowed you to come and see us." Mrs Bennet's usual piercing tones were subdued to an almost inaudible whisper.

"I do not think he ever intended to stop us visiting you, Mama," said Elizabeth gently. "We are all bound for Derbyshire on Thursday, and Jane and I would like you to come help us choose our wedding clothes." Surely this, if anything, would rouse her mother.

Mrs Bennet hardly seemed to hear. "He was very angry yesterday. He shouted at me. He has never shouted at me before." She lowered her voice still further. "I think he had been drinking."

"Mama!"

"I do not understand why he was so angry. He has never said anything before about the way I was raising you all. If he did not like it, why did he not say something before? It is not fair to be angry now."

Elizabeth took her mother's cold hand in hers and chafed it. "No, Mama. It is not fair."

"I was so happy that you and Jane were to be married and you were going to be rich and…and…safe. And then he came and shouted at me."

Elizabeth glanced helplessly at Jane, who was so much better at this sort of thing than she was. Jane came over and took her place, murmuring the soft-voiced reassurances that were all their mother needed at this time. She was in no fit state for any rational examination of her predicament; she needed the comfort Jane was the best person to supply.

Elizabeth went over to Lydia's bed. Here was another who looked distinctly unwell. She had always been a plump, healthy sort of girl, but now her face looked grey and puffy. She was pathetically glad to see first her sisters and then their aunt Gardiner, who came in with tea a few minutes later.

They saw Lydia drink her tea and then settle down for a rest after Elizabeth and Jane both promised not to leave before she woke. Mrs Gardiner took Elizabeth into another room while Jane settled their mother down for a rest and undertook to stay with her. She was still holding her mother's hand and comforting her when they left.

Elizabeth had always been a favourite of Mr and Mrs Gardiner, and before they turned to more unpleasant matters, Mrs Gardiner congratulated her niece on her engagement with all the generous enthusiasm of her nature. "I do not speak only of his position and means," she said. "He is a man of superior understanding and genuine charity towards those less fortunate than himself." She smiled; she was only a few years older than her niece. "And he is also extremely handsome, which is hardly ever a bad thing in a husband."

"I know," replied Elizabeth. "And the best of it is he hardly seems to notice it himself."

They both sighed happily before getting down to less pleasant business.

"Your father was already agitated when he arrived," Mrs Gardiner began. "Unfortunately, although I do not wish to be unkind, your mother was in high spirits about you and Jane and…well, inclined to pass off Lydia's situation as soon to be sorted, whereupon you and Jane would find *her* a rich husband too."

Oh, Mama, thought Elizabeth.

"Lydia joined in the speculation, and it soon became obvious that she had no idea what childbirth would represent nor even how long she should expect to be confined." Mrs Gardiner looked distressed. "I am certain, truly certain, that her remarks were born of ignorance. The poor child seems to know very little, not even those details thought suitable for genteel young ladies, but the effect was deeply improper. I am afraid I was glad the children were all at my mother's house for the weekend."

"And my father became angry."

"Lizzy, he became furious. Although I did not think it at all likely, I believe your mother was afraid he might strike her." This was worse than Elizabeth had suspected, and worst of all, she had no idea what, if anything, she could do about the situation. She was bitterly angry with her father. Once again, she felt as though she were being asked to make decisions and settle differences that were not hers to make or settle. She was about to ask her aunt what she ought to do when she suddenly realised there was someone else with whom she could share the burden. She would not always have Jane and Aunt Gardiner to advise and console, but *he* would share all her worries, take up all her battles, and count himself blessed to be able to do so.

She was about to say something of this to Mrs Gardiner when a cry came from her mother and Lydia's room.

"Auntie!" It was almost a scream, and when they rushed into the room, they found Jane and Mrs Bennet staring in horror at Lydia, who had thrown back her bedclothes to reveal her nightgown and a growing scarlet stain.

When she looked back on the next few hours, Elizabeth found that she had only a confused memory of a doctor (short, fat, and peremptory but deft and gentle), Lydia (sobbing and screaming), Mrs Bennet (roused and surprisingly steadfast), stained linen, and the smell of laudanum and blood.

At one stage, they feared for Lydia's life and sent for their father, but by the time he arrived, all seemed to have taken a happier turn, and although the child was lost, Lydia's life was spared.

Mr Bennet or, indeed, any man had no place in this sick room, and since his wife was busy with Lydia and refused to come down, he left for Grosvenor Square as soon as it became obvious that the worst had not happened. Elizabeth and Jane stayed longer, comforting Lydia and helping their aunt and the servants set the room to rights. First Lydia and then Mrs Bennet fell asleep, and Elizabeth and Jane went downstairs to wash and take a light supper.

By the time they set off in the carriage, which had returned after leaving Mr Bennet at Darcy House, it was almost nine o'clock, and they were exhausted. By the time they arrived home, they were almost asleep.

To Elizabeth's delight, Mr Darcy was waiting for her in the hall. To Jane's delight, he held a letter for her from Mr Bingley, brought by courier only an hour before. Suddenly awake, she seized it joyfully and hurried upstairs to read.

They both smiled as they watched her disappear around the corner, and then he turned to her and gestured towards the drawing room. "Are you too tired to talk awhile?"

She shook her head. "I believe I am too tired not to." Then, when he raised an eyebrow, she added, "You are a necessity to me now, sir. I cannot do without you." She thought he would have kissed her then had they not been in so public a place. They went into the sitting room. A fire had been lit, and she was glad of it, so she sat in a chair close by, trying and failing not to blush when she rested her feet on a pretty little stool.

"Would you like some tea? Or, I know, what about chocolate?" She nodded gratefully and sank back into her chair, watching as he summoned a servant and gave his order; then, to her surprise, he poured a small glass of brandy and offered it to her. "It can help," he said. "Especially if one is tired and fears one will be unable to sleep."

She took it and cradled it in her hand, bringing it to her nose for she had always loved the smell, before taking a small sip.

"How is Miss Lydia?"

"Tired and distressed, but I think she will do well. The doctor was very reassuring. I had no idea such things were so common."

"I have written to Pemberley to delay our arrival. You must tell me when we are able to make the journey." She was grateful. and said so, but she could not help but show how little such a delay was to her taste. The chocolate arrived, hot and creamy—a childhood treat appearing like a miracle on a day when she felt she had left her childhood behind forever.

"How did you know?" she asked.

"Georgiana always wants chocolate when she feels sad or unwell."

She drank, and the warmth of the drink and the warmth of the brandy seemed to loosen something inside her, the urge to keep things private suddenly gone like a pair of shoes she had outgrown.

"Do you ever think about your parents, Fitzwilliam?"

He looked a little surprised but answered readily enough. "Recently more and more. I think it has taken me too long to realise that they were merely men and women like ourselves, just as fallible, just as…human. I spent many years attempting to live up to the man I thought my father was, only to find he was something quite different, something not necessarily, or at least not entirely, admirable. What made you ask?"

She told him what she had learned and became angry once more in the telling. "You know what my mother is. Her understanding is not strong and likely never has been, but he is a clever man. He must have seen what she was about all these years. It is too harsh, too cruel to burden her with the full weight of responsibility for Lydia's imprudence, and all at once in one angry outburst."

He sat opposite her, taking her hands in his, running his thumbs over the backs in the way she found so comforting. "I cannot but agree," he replied. "Even though we both know that, in too many families, raising the children is wholly the mother's occupation, the children rarely appearing to their fathers at all. My own father spoke to me only once or twice a week until I was thirteen or fourteen years of age. Many fathers would do the same."

"But not you," she said with confidence.

"No," he agreed. "Not me. And as for the harshness…" He shrugged. "It is not easy for anyone, least of all the master of a house, to confront his own inadequacies. As you say, he is a clever man. He cannot but be aware of all this."

Elizabeth looked into the depths of her chocolate cup; this, at least, she found embarrassing. "She is afraid of him now— physically afraid. I am not sure I can forgive that, nor am I sure I want him at my wedding…"

There was a sound in the open doorway leading to the library. They turned towards it and found Mr Bennet standing there, the volume of Aeschylus in his hand.

For a moment no one moved or spoke. Then Mr Bennet turned on his heel and left. Elizabeth half rose to follow him then subsided into her chair. Darcy took her hand. "I think you are wise, my dear," he said. "If he were willing to speak, he would have stayed. Perhaps tomorrow when emotions have calmed…"

"I fear we Bennets are not displaying ourselves to advantage," said Elizabeth unhappily.

"Then it is fortunate that I am marrying one Bennet who is." He kissed the hand he held. "You must be exhausted. I do not want you to go, but you really should rest. I know you will want to return to Gracechurch Street tomorrow." He paused and looked a little uneasy. "Would you like me to accompany you?"

He still held her hand, so this time she lifted his hand and gently kissed the knuckles. "I wish you could, but we both know that no one else will want you there." She looked up at him. "Promise me we shall leave for Pemberley the moment it is possible, wedding clothes or not."

"I promise." He pulled her gently to her feet, and they embraced, his arms round her shoulders, hers round his waist before she left to make her weary way upstairs. Her maid was waiting and must have been warned of her exhaustion for her nightgown was ready, a brick warming the sheets of the luxurious bed, and she was undressed and asleep within minutes.

CHAPTER 23

ARRANGING THINGS TO HIS SATISFACTION

NEXT MORNING, THE BENNET SISTERS MET IN ELIZABETH'S room before breakfast, and Jane had the unpleasant task of explaining to Mary and Kitty what had happened to Lydia. In view of their mother's reaction to Mr Bennet's comments, Elizabeth believed she had no choice but to share with them something of what had happened in that regard. Both were shocked, even Mary's moralising was silenced, and it was a quiet group that came down to breakfast a little before nine.

As the butler led them to the family dining room, they heard their uncle Gardiner's furious voice as he entered the library. "For heaven's sake, Bennet," he said. "You knew what she was when you married her. What possessed you..." Then the door closed, and they heard no more. Kitty began to cry, and Jane led her back upstairs to compose herself.

Georgiana and Mr Darcy were taking breakfast when they arrived, and Elizabeth was deeply thankful that they were behind enough closed doors to have kept Mr Gardiner's voice from them. Georgiana said enough by way of enquiry after Lydia to reveal that she had not been told the nature of her illness, and Elizabeth resolved to warn her sisters.

"I have ordered the carriage for half past ten," said Darcy. "I hope that is convenient."

"Yes, thank you."

"Do Miss Mary and Miss Catherine accompany you?"

"They are both anxious to see Lydia and our mother. I doubt we shall be back until evening. I shall send word as soon as I know what we are about."

Gracechurch Street was a happier place than it had been the previous day if only because the children had returned and were delighted to see all their cousins at once. Amidst the clinging arms, demands for stories, and insistent descriptions of their recent stay with their grandmother, Elizabeth had some difficulty escaping to visit their mother and Lydia.

Lydia was pale and tired but, thanks no doubt in part to her youth, seemed on the way back to health. The doctor had visited already, pronounced himself pleased with her recovery, and that, should it proceed as expected, Lydia could travel within a fortnight or so. In the meantime, she was to rest. Mrs Bennet, while no longer as quiet as she had been, was much more subdued than usual and seemed content to stay with Lydia and see to her comfort.

When Lydia fell asleep shortly after luncheon and visits from Mary and Kitty, Elizabeth and Jane took their mother aside and attempted to discover her thoughts. To their horror, they found that she expected she and Mr Bennet would separate and merely hoped that, wherever she was to be settled, she would be allowed to see her daughters.

"For Mr Bennet was so very angry at how you girls were brought up that I am sure he will not want me to have anything more to do with you all."

"Oh, Mama. I promise you, there will be at least two daughters who will not be denied you." It was, reflected Elizabeth, something of a reversal for her to be taking her mother's part against her father, and while she did not wish her mother to feel deserted by them all, she could not deny that a part of her was horrified at the idea that Mrs Bennet might expect to come and live with her and Mr Darcy at Pemberley. She attempted to chide herself for her lack of charity and failed miserably.

It was all the more gratifying, therefore, when Mr Gardiner returned with happier news. Although he refused to discuss the details with his nieces, he gave them to understand that a reconciliation of sorts had been arranged. There would be no separation but neither would they be returning to Meryton for a while. Instead, a house had been rented in Scarborough for the period of Lydia's recuperation, and they would repair there after the weddings. Mrs Annesley, who believed herself superfluous now that Mr Darcy was marrying, was to go with them to act as both governess and guide, and Mrs Bennet had undertaken not to interfere with any guidance she might give.

Elizabeth had a suspicion as to who had suggested this solution and, indeed, who was probably paying for it since a chance remark some days ago had hinted that Mrs Annesley's services were somewhat expensive. However, in the general heartfelt relief, she did not feel obliged to ask—nor, she realised, did she greatly care.

When they got back to Darcy House after dining at Gracechurch Street, she found her father had already gone to bed, and it was not long before Mary, Kitty, and Jane went up too. Mr Darcy, however, was waiting for her, and he had a letter from her father.

With some trepidation, she followed him into the sitting room, saw that all doors were closed, sat down before the fire, and opened her letter.

My Dear Child,
I cannot deny I was shocked by your words last night. I hope you
know that I would never strike your mother or any lady. However,
also I cannot deny I was greatly disturbed by what I found when
I visited your mother and Lydia on Sunday night. In all their

foolish plans, neither of them seemed aware that Lydia can never expect to marry any gentleman of fortune, or indeed any gentleman of ordinary prudence, and refused to believe me when I attempted to explain.

It was this more than anything that revealed to me the extent to which Lydia's education (and no doubt that of Kitty and perhaps Mary too) has failed to give her any true understanding of morality or even ordinary propriety. I was extremely angry with your mother, of course, but also with myself. As your young man pointed out, my own failure was perhaps even harder to swallow.

It is easy to make promises of amendment, although somewhat harder to do so to one's own daughter, and it is even harder to keep them. However, I fully intend to take a greater part in the education of my remaining daughters in the hope that they will turn out half as well as you and Jane.

Your loving father,
Thomas Bennet

She sighed wearily and handed the letter to Darcy. "Do you think he can be trusted?"

He read it, and she loved that he would not rush into easy reassurances. "Indolence is perhaps the hardest habit to break, but we can always intervene later should it prove necessary." He handed back the letter.

"And after all, we have a spy in the camp now." He barely had time to blush before she added, "Do not think that I am complaining. If Mrs Annesley is willing, it is an excellent solution." She smiled. "And one worthy of my Machiavellian betrothed."

He bent over her chair and kissed her swiftly on the lips. "I prefer to think of myself as prudent."

"Cunning."

He kissed her again. "Far-sighted."

"Manipulative."

That one did bring him up short. "Do you really think so? I am attempting to abandon the habit of arranging other people's lives without their consent. I trust I have not failed at this early juncture."

"I suspect my father and uncle were well aware of what was happening." She shrugged and watched in surprise as, for some reason, that made him shiver and clasp his hands behind his back. "And even if they were not, I must confess that I am glad of any solution that does not involve my mama coming to live with us." She looked up at him: half-laughing, half-anxious. "Does that make me a bad person?"

He looked at her for a moment, his expression tender. Then, to her surprise, he walked behind her. She twisted in her chair to look, only to blush and twist back when she saw what he was carrying.

He set the footstool before her chair and lifted her bodily, and with exciting ease, so that she stood upon it. Then, standing before her, he brushed her hair from her forehead, for in the course of a long day it had escaped its pins, took her head in his hands, and kissed her once.

"No, my love. It makes you human." He kissed her again. "And delightful." He kissed her again. "And if you wish to continue these private interviews, please refrain from shrugging your shoulders when I am standing over you. The view is extremely provocative, and I, too, am only human."

He laughed when she looked down to see what he meant, but when she looked up, he kissed her again and then again. His mouth was hot and wet, and she twined her arms round his neck, raking the fingers of one hand through his curls. He made a sound deep in his throat and pressed her closer, one warm hand in the small of her back. Heat poured off him and into her as she slid her tongue over and about his. Her legs were trembling, and when one of his hands smoothed up over the muslin of her gown and touched her breast, they gave way altogether.

He caught her as she would have fallen and set her back in her chair. Then he knelt before her, gathered her hands in his and rested his forehead on them. She was breathing as though she had been running, and so was he, but it was not until she began to feel chilled and shivered that he looked up. "I have not frightened you?" he said.

"I feel I ought to answer yes—but no, I am not afraid of you. I am a little afraid of *us*, but only because this is all so new. Is it always like this?"

"I do not know. It has never been like this before, but then it has never been love before; it has never been you before."

She considered that for a moment. "I have always known...I mean you are a gentleman, and gentlemen are considered different, and I knew there might have been..." She paused helplessly. "I don't know any polite words."

"There are very few polite words. Elizabeth, I cannot claim that I was not as foolish as most young men. I was." He kissed her hand again. "But I was never a libertine, even at my most foolish. It was never..." He, too, was groping for words. "It was never at the expense of any woman's peace of mind or future happiness. And now there is you, and it will only ever be you."

"Even when I have grown fat and ugly bearing your children?"

He smiled fondly. "So you have decided we are going to have children now?"

"Not if you don't immediately reassure me that bearing them will not alter your regard."

"I promise faithfully to become more besotted with each child." His smile faded, and he swallowed. "I should dearly like to kiss you again, dearest, but I think I had better not."

"Perhaps you are right." She stood up and shook out her skirts as he leaned back upon his heels and smiled up at her. "But there is no reason why I should not kiss you." So she bent down, kissed him on the nose and ran out of the room before he could regain his feet.

CHAPTER 24

WEDDING GIFTS

"GOOD GRIEF!"

He did not think he had ever seen anything quite this hideous in his entire life. Compared to this...this...thing, even the portrait of his great-great-grandfather Walter looked vaguely acceptable. He circled it warily, wondering how on earth he was going to explain this to Elizabeth, or indeed anyone with any vestige of normal taste.

"Mr Bingley, sir." He could have sworn even Broadbent's voice trembled.

Bingley bounded into the library, only to stop dead when he saw what was currently occupying the desktop. "My God!" He, too, stared in appalled fascination. "And I thought the china my Aunt Matilda sent us was hideous!"

"No, that was merely ugly. I fancy this is Plato's Form of Hideousness—the archetypal hideousness from which all mortal hideousness derives." He was, Darcy realised, rather enjoying himself.

Bingley inspected it again. "Is that lion really eating the unfortunate native gentleman?"

"I sincerely hope so. The alternative does not bear contemplation." There was a snort from behind the desk, and they looked up to see a mortified footman, obviously biting inside his mouth to stop himself laughing. "That will be all, Bateman. You can clear the crate and straw away later. Please tell Miss Bennet that Mr Bingley has called."

Bingley circled the desk. "Who on earth would send you that? I mean it is obviously expensive but…well, look at it…"

"It is a wedding present from my great-uncle Darcy." He sighed. "I think it is an epergne, but it is certainly nothing one could have on one's dining table. Whichever way you turn it, someone is going to spend their entire meal staring at an elephant's hindquarters."

"You think those are elephants?"

"Don't you?"

Miss Bennet and Miss Elizabeth arrived at this point although their attempts to greet their respective intendeds trailed into silence.

"What do you think the tall thing in the middle is supposed to represent?" asked Elizabeth after a few moments of silent appreciation.

They all looked at it.

"I suspect it is a giraffe rendered by someone who had never actually seen a giraffe," said Darcy eventually.

"I have never seen a giraffe, but I am fairly certain they do not look like that!" To everyone's surprise, this was Jane Bennet, and it was hard to tell who was most surprised by the comment. It was not at all like her to express so unguarded an opinion.

"Never seen a giraffe? We must do something about that. They still have one at the Tower menagerie, do they not, Darcy?" Bingley did not wait for a reply. "We shall go and inspect it at once." Within ten minutes, Bingley, Miss Bennet, and a somewhat reluctant Mary were bound for the Tower in a Darcy carriage Bingley had heartlessly appropriated for his own use, doubtless because he was desperate for a little time in relative privacy with his bride-to-be.

"I feel somewhat guilty about Bingley and Miss Bennet," said Darcy, as he watched them go. "You realise they should have been married by now?"

"I do not think it was any of your doing. If anyone is to blame, surely it is Lydia."

"Still, I know if it were my wedding that had been so unceremoniously postponed…" They shared a look that made them both flush and turned hurriedly to look at the wedding present.

Elizabeth peered into the crate. "There is a letter in here."

The handwriting was feminine—the letter, direct.

Foss House, The Pavement
York

Dear Nephew,
I was glad to get your letter. Your father and I quarrelled, but that was so long ago I can hardly remember why, and in any event, since you are my only living relative and I have no idea how long I have left, it seems foolish to keep the estrangement going.

I have sent you one of the presents your aunt Clara and I got when we wed. It was from her uncle the nabob. I have had fifty years' entertainment out of it. The number of idiots who will compliment you on it is truly astounding, and I am still not certain what some of the animals are supposed to be. Your aunt always swore there was a hedgehog in there somewhere.

You did not say much about your wife in your letter, but what you did say reminded me of my Clara so, once the honeymoon is over, I should like to invite you to bring her to York to see me. There's only my poor boy's wife and me here now, but we can still make you welcome.

Your affect. uncle,
James Darcy.

Then underneath, in a much fainter, more crabbed hand.

People talk a lot of damned nonsense about marriage, but if you can marry a friend, as I did—someone you can talk to—then you will do better than most.

Then underneath, even fainter.

Take my advice: never try to hide anything from your wife. They always find out in the end.

Elizabeth handed him back the letter. "He sounds like a delightful old gentleman. Do say we can visit him."

Darcy kissed her hand, made ridiculously happy by her choice of pronoun. They were going to be a 'we.'

"I am yours to command, madam," he replied and had to clear his throat.

"I shall remember that, sir." He put out a hand to touch her cheek, and she seized it in both of hers. "Two weeks—it is only two weeks," she said and then had to laugh at his doleful expression. "I must go. I have an appointment with a mantua-maker so very exclusive I am almost afraid I shall need Almack's vouchers to be admitted as a customer."

"Who goes with you?"

"Mama, Georgie, and Mrs Annesley. We are to meet my aunt Gardiner there." She glanced up at him, and he thought she looked a little anxious. "You know I cannot exclude Mama. It would be too cruel."

"Of course you must take her. I was merely concerned it might precipitate further conflict with your father." He could have kicked himself when she looked down and away from him.

"I have spoken to Papa and have his agreement," she said

unhappily. "We are at least conversing once more; however, I am not sure we shall ever be the friends we once were."

"At least you had his friendship when you were growing up. I for one shall always be grateful he esteemed and made much of you. Perhaps you should try to remember that rather than more recent events."

He paused for a moment and seemed to be gathering something—courage perhaps?—before he continued. "My own father had little time for me until I was old enough to be of use. Had it not been for my grandmother Darcy, I suspect I should have had a very isolated childhood. You know I was ill as a child?" She nodded. "It was Grandmother who sat with me hour after hour, reading and singing to me." He smiled and began to sing softly,

> *"Where have you been all the day, Billy boy, Billy boy?*
> *Where have you been all the day, my Billy boy?*
> *I've been walking all the day, with a lady fine and gay*
> *And my Nancy is my fancy,*
> *Though she's young to leave her mother,*
> *She's the only wife for me."*

Elizabeth smiled fondly and sang back to him

> *"Is she fit to be your wife, Billy boy, Billy boy?*
> *Is she fit to be your wife, my Billy boy?"*

To which he replied,

> *"She's as fit to be my wife as the fork is to the knife,*
> *And my Nancy is my fancy,*
> *Though she's young to leave her mother,*
> *She's the only wife for me."*

He would have kissed her then, but as he leaned down and she leaned up, the clock struck eleven. She gave a little cry of alarm and ran out of the library.

Elizabeth might have found the opulent surroundings of Madam Clothilde's (née Mary Ramsbottom's) establishment somewhat daunting had it not been for the presence of Georgie and Mrs Gardiner—the former because she was so obviously accustomed to the attention and accepted it as no more than her due and that of her brother's wife, the latter because her calm good taste made the task of choosing the excessive number of gowns apparently necessary in her new station in life so much easier. As gown followed gown and silk followed figured muslin, Elizabeth began to wonder who was going to pay for all this, the furs they were to buy tomorrow, and the toilet articles she was to shop for the following day. Especially since she soon realised that a considerable premium had been promised to ensure delivery before they all left for Derbyshire.

Luckily, Aunt Gardiner realised where her thoughts were tending. "Elizabeth," she said with fond exasperation, "you must allow the people who love you to spoil you on occasion. I have had strict instructions from your father, your uncle, and Mr Darcy, all quite separately, that no expense is to be spared."

"But—"

"But me no buts, Niece. When a gentleman has set his heart upon spoiling you, there is nothing to be done save to let him. It gives him pleasure to please you, and that is not a habit you wish to discourage." Over her aunt's head, Elizabeth could see Madam Clothilde nodding emphatically.

So Elizabeth cast aside her worries and determined to enjoy the experience, although she was careful to secure Madam Ramsbottom's (alias Clothilde's) assurances that the seamstresses would receive a substantial share of the premium that was being paid. She supposed a time would come when such things would become commonplace, but for the moment, there was something delightful in not having to choose only one of two materials presented to her, while matching ribbons and buttons were all at hand instead of requiring time-consuming trips about town.

However, if Elizabeth enjoyed the experience, it was nothing to the joy it brought her mother. Unlike her daughter, and to Elizabeth's relief, she was overawed by the establishment and seemed content to sit, sipping tea, her eyes shining as she drank in the experience as greedily as she consumed the tea and cakes. Once or twice she ventured a suggestion, usually in favour of more ornamentation, but seemed quite happy to accept Madame Clothilde's assurances that, "Mademoiselle does not 'ave ze, 'ow you say, 'eight to carry off ze more elaborate creations."

Elizabeth had always considered her mother insatiable, for she had never seemed content no matter what was done for or about her. As Elizabeth slipped in and out of half-sewn forms, pored over pattern books, and inspected bolts of cloth, she realised that her mother was as happy as any child in a sweet-shop, the only difference lying in the fact that this was an unselfish joy. For what felt like the first time in Elizabeth's life, her mother was happy for and because of her. Mrs Bennet neither wanted nor expected anything for herself. She was utterly content watching her daughter being treated in a manner she had hitherto thought reserved for royalty.

Elizabeth was touched and, for the first time in many years, remembered her mother as a young woman, dancing with them in the nursery and singing to her babies as she dressed them in clothes the young Fanny Gardiner had always wanted and had never been able to afford. She knew this silent joy was unlikely to last but made a vow to herself that she would never forget this moment: her mother surrounded by bolts of silk, delirious with happiness.

After a long day, which was concluded with celebratory ices at Gunter's, they all returned to Darcy House, exhausted but happy. Even the prospect of a family dinner with Mr Bennet had been insufficient to spoil the afternoon for Mrs Bennet, and when Darcy re-entered his library before dinner, he found his future mother-in-law standing next to Elizabeth, starting in raptures at Great-Uncle James's wedding present.

"Oh, Mr Darcy, what a magnificent...article," said Mrs Bennet, and Darcy and Elizabeth had to avoid catching each other's eye for the rest of the evening.

CHAPTER 25

UNDER SOCIETY'S GAZE

NEXT DAY, DARCY INSISTED ON ACCOMPANYING HER TO THE furriers. He did not trust anyone else to ensure that Elizabeth was provided with the very best. Georgie came along for propriety's sake and was of tremendous help in persuading Elizabeth that what he wanted her to have was no more than was appropriate. She still protested a little, but in the end, he had the satisfaction of seeing Elizabeth in a magnificent sable cloak, the hood framing her face as she laughed, half-embarrassed, half-awed, twisting and turning before the mirrors in innocent enjoyment of her own appearance.

That night, he dreamed he made her his on that sable, her skin luminous against the blackness: silk, velvet, and fur. He woke embarrassed as he had not been in over a dozen years.

The week before they were due to leave for Derbyshire, he took her to the opera. Bingley and Jane were due to dine with the Hursts, and Mr Bennet quoted Doctor Johnson, calling opera an 'irrational and exotic entertainment,' and refused to attend, so the party was confined to Darcy, Elizabeth, and Georgiana.

It was the first occasion she had worn one of her new gowns, a lovely creation of ivory silk with dark red embroidery. Georgie must have told him what she was to wear because, before Elizabeth came down, he sent Georgie into her room with the family rubies. She stared at them for several minutes, scarcely daring to touch—a magnificent necklace of smaller stones to circle the throat before falling to a central stone of such fiery brilliance that the eye was irresistibly drawn to it.

"Oh, Georgie, I cannot," she breathed.

"If you do not, no one else will," said Georgiana sensibly, and not really reluctant, Elizabeth was persuaded.

The look on his face when she came down the main staircase convinced her she had done the right thing. He did not smile, but his eyes were shining as he bent over her gloved hand. "You look beautiful, my dear," he said softly as he tucked her arm into his.

"I feel beautiful," she replied as they climbed into the coach. "And I feel I ought to thank you for it. For, with Jane as a sister, it is not a sensation to which I am accustomed." As they passed through crowded streets to the theatre, she could see he looked faintly uneasy and reflected how much easier it was becoming to discern his thoughts and reactions.

"Will you tell me why you are concerned, Fitzwilliam?" she said. "I am assuming it has nothing to do with my appearance."

She could see that she had surprised him. "Of course not," he replied. "It is just difficult to explain without sounding like a complete coxcomb." He sighed and ran a hand through his hair. "It is just that I fear we shall attract a certain amount of attention at the theatre. My matrimonial prospects have been the subject of so much speculation since I reached my majority that people will want to see who I am to marry. Some of the attention will be ill-bred, and I apologise for it."

"I am sure it can be no worse than Mrs Long and my aunt Philips."

"In those cases, there was at least a foundation of goodwill towards you. I cannot guarantee the same will be the case in this instance."

Elizabeth considered this for a moment then shook her head firmly. "As I informed you at your aunt Catherine's piano, my courage rises with every attempt to intimidate me. If London society does not wish for my acquaintance, I shall have to console myself with the fact that you and Georgie do. I have a high enough opinion of my own deserts to be satisfied with that."

She turned to Georgiana. "I just hope it will not spoil your enjoyment of the theatre."

He sat back and watched her as she engaged his sister in conversation, appreciating the consideration that sought to ease Georgiana's already lively fear of appearing in public. The jewels about her throat sparkled as she turned between Georgiana, himself, and the carriage windows, and his eye was caught by the creamy expanse of skin on which the great ruby lay and the soft swell of her bosom. The next day they were to leave for Pemberley, and three days after that, they were to be wed. He would stand beside her in the church at Lambton, she would become his forever, and he would dedicate himself to her happiness and well-being. He dare not consider beyond that, for his dreams were becoming insistent, and it was all he could do sometimes not to seize her to his heart and touch and kiss and know.

She and Georgie were talking of childhood visits to the theatre, and although he knew Elizabeth was not quite as at ease as she might wish, he also knew that she genuinely did not see why she should be daunted. Her gloved hands were white in the gloom of the carriage, and he watched them dart about as she reduced his sister to helpless giggles describing her first visit to the pantomime as a very small child when, outraged by the clown's behaviour, she had had to be prevented from climbing on the stage to berate him for his treatment of his poor 'wife'.

The carriage joined the queue before the theatre doors, and he could see the lights and the press of people up ahead. He had always hated the display, the parade before curious eyes, the attempts to attract his attention or interest. He went to the opera for the music and sometimes wondered whether he was the only person who did. Tonight, for the first time, he thought that he would not mind the impertinence. Tonight, Elizabeth would be on his arm, and he was so very proud of her. The carriage finally stopped, and he got out first, turning to give her his hand. The lamps and torches burned bright enough to make his eyes smart, but they were no brighter than she was, climbing out of his carriage, her eyes interested and alert, her gloved hands deft with her gown and stole.

As Georgiana stepped out behind them, Elizabeth turned and took her arm. "Come, Georgie," she said. "You can show me where to go. The sooner we have done with the 'irrational' part of the evening's proceedings, the sooner we can begin the 'exotic'."

He followed them up the stairs and into the foyer, his heart bursting with pride. Heads turned, gossips of both sexes anxious to miss nothing. He exchanged bows with one or two people he knew, but they were merely a distraction from the sight of *her*. There were mirrors on the walls, and he was faintly disconcerted to see that he was not sporting a grin every bit as foolish as any he had accused Bingley of wearing. He looked no different, and it felt to him as though he ought. He was a different man—strange that it was not visible. He shrugged mentally and clasped his hands behind his back as he followed the two women he loved into his box.

In a box opposite, Lady Grosvenor, one of Lady Catherine's cronies, was giving him the quizzing-glass. He smiled sweetly, bowed, and had the satisfaction of seeing her look away. Georgie was looking at him a little worriedly, so he patted her arm. "Do not be alarmed, Georgie, m'duck," he said happily. "I have merely decided that society has only as much consequence as we choose to grant it. You look delightful, Elizabeth looks delightful, the music should be excellent, and really, what else do we need for an evening at the theatre?"

Georgie appeared doubtful, but as she and Elizabeth settled into their seats, shook out their skirts, and got out their opera glasses and libretti, he had the satisfaction of feeling comfortable under the gaze of half of society for the first time in his life. If they did not appreciate Elizabeth, then that was decidedly their loss. So long as they kept their opinions to themselves, he was quite prepared to consign them to the ▬ and enjoy himself. The overture struck up; Mozart, scurrying, and dancing. He heard Elizabeth laughing softly in delight and sat back to watch her enjoyment.

People did come to visit during the intervals—men with whom he had been to Cambridge, some quite obviously dragged there by their curious wives, a couple of Derbyshire neighbours, friends of his or Fitzwilliam or Uncle Matlock— but all in all, it was not so bad. Elizabeth was more than capable of looking after herself on the rare occasion when it proved necessary. He loved her ease in company, her ability to take and give compliments, her refusal to be condescended to. He laughed to himself as he heard her cheerfully agreeing with Lady Walgrave that no one had ever heard of her or her family while subtly implying that being known was perhaps a trifle… vulgar? Faversham came—corseted, painted, a little ridiculous, but at heart a decent fellow—and Darcy managed to slip into the conversation that his uncle Matlock had met Elizabeth and approved. That should ensure the news was passed round the circles where such things were considered important. As the final act began, he realised that it was possibly the most comfortable evening he had ever had at the theatre. Even his sister looked less petrified and had been tempted into a few quiet words about the quality of the singing.

As the music wound to its ecstatic climax, he took Elizabeth's hand beneath the rim of the box. She turned and flashed him a brilliant smile, and his heart turned over. He wished he had the words, he wished they were alone so that he could say them, but they were not, and perhaps it did not matter, for she squeezed his hand and nodded.

"*Ah, tutti contenti, saremo cosi.*" The voices on stage rose and fell, and it seemed to him that only great art such as this could possibly describe the emotions that swelled within him. Dazed by his own happiness, he hardly noticed when the music ended and they found coats and wraps and prepared to leave. This time, he insisted on offering both women an arm, even though they quite blocked the staircase to the foyer. Young Tom was waiting there to show them to their carriage. Elizabeth was humming the penultimate chorus, her eyes dreamy. One day soon they would come here as man and wife, and if they wished to sit side by side and hold hands, then no one would be able to gainsay them.

It was very late when they arrived back at Darcy House, and Georgie was dozing in one corner. He had so managed things that Elizabeth was sitting beside him, and gradually, as they filed through the crowd of carriages, she had come to rest her head on his arm. One day soon, he would be able to put that arm around her. One day soon, he would be able to kiss her if he wanted to, though not perhaps if they had company. He made a mental note to be certain that Georgie was not neglected on that account.

Footmen were waiting with torches, and the doors stood open as they climbed out of the carriage. Georgie was yawning on his arm. Suddenly, a man darted out of the blackness. Instinctively, Darcy thrust his sister behind him and stepped in front of Elizabeth. The man was carrying a short club or stick with a brass crown on the end.

"Fitzwilliam Darcy," he said in a gruff, uneducated voice. "I am a tipstaff and you are served."

With that he tapped Darcy on the shoulder with a long

thin bundle of papers that he dropped on the ground. He was gone before the footmen had time to react.

Darcy bent down and picked up the papers as Elizabeth hustled Georgie inside. 'Ephraim Hollernshaw MP v Fitzwilliam Darcy Esquire,' it read. 'Writ of Criminal Conversation.'

CHAPTER 26

OBSTACLES IN THE ROAD

WHEN ELIZABETH CAME DOWNSTAIRS AFTER SETTLING Georgiana in her chamber, she had to ask a servant Mr Darcy's whereabouts. She was directed to his study where she found him at his desk, still in the coat he had worn at the theatre complete with the complex edifice that was his neck-cloth. The room was dark, save for the lamps about the desk, and the silk about his throat seemed to shine.

He was so intent on whatever it was he was writing that he did not hear her enter; she had to call his name. His expression when he looked up was every bit as forbidding as it had ever been at the beginning of their acquaintance. She refused to be daunted. "What has happened?" she said.

His voice was even as he replied. "I am accused of adultery. The husband seeks damages."

"No." She stared at him, aghast. She remembered his admission of past indiscretion and for a moment wondered if that past had returned to revenge itself. Then, as she approached the desk, she got a proper view of his face. There was no guilt. There was not even any consciousness of past actions. There was merely anger, a bitter, deadly rage that, even though she knew it was not directed at her, she still found somewhat frightening.

"Tell me," she said.

"The lady is the sister of my late friend Richard, Lord Meopham." Briefly, he outlined the history of his dealings with Mrs Hollernshaw and the trust placed in him by his friend. "Obviously, Mr Hollernshaw has discovered the legacy. This action is an impudent attempt to extort the property for his own use. The amount of damages claimed is approximately equivalent to the value of the estate, and he obviously expects me to make it over to him to avoid scandal." He turned back to his letter as though he considered the conversation at an end.

"What are you going to do?"

"I am going to ruin him." It was not said with any particular emphasis, but Elizabeth did not doubt him. "This is the action of a stupid and desperate man. Whatever drove him to this, I shall discover it and use it to destroy him." He finished one letter, drew another sheet towards him, and began another.

"Fitzwilliam?" Either he did not hear or he did not wish to hear, so she came round to his side of the desk and forced him to acknowledge her. "This will not prevent us from leaving tomorrow...?"

He would not meet her eyes. "This is going to be difficult and distasteful. I do not wish you to be involved."

"And what about what I want?"

He did not seem to hear her. "I shall speak to your father tomorrow. Now that Miss Lydia's situation is no longer pressing, we can wait until I have dealt with this matter."

She seized his face between her hands and forced him to meet her gaze. "Fitzwilliam, I do not care about any of this. I love you. I want to marry you." Then, seeing his set expression, she felt the wreck of all her hopes. "You promised!"

"Elizabeth, you must allow that I know more of the world than—" She pressed her lips to his, stopping his words, forcing her tongue into his mouth. He tried to turn his head, but she sank her fingers into his hair. For a few seconds, she thought she had gained ascendancy until he forced her hands free, rose to his feet and backed away. He was breathing heavily, his face pale.

"There is more at stake here than anything you or I may desire," he said. "One of the allegations is that Mrs Hollernshaw and I held clandestine meetings in an hotel in Ramsgate. I was there at the time although I had no knowledge of her presence." He swallowed and looked away. "I was with Georgiana, but I cannot and will not distress her by explaining why we were there, not to you and certainly not in open court."

He turned to face her. "I am faced with many difficulties. I have to extricate myself from this charge without stain to my character, without acceding to his demands, and without worsening Mrs Hollernshaw's situation. The evidence he claims to hold is false, the witnesses suborned, but I have no way of assessing how the case will stand in court. I shall fight, but I cannot disguise from you that I may lose."

"Then let me help. Let me stand beside you and proclaim to the world the falsity of these allegations." She was standing before him now, her hands grasping his lapels, her face upturned to his, and almost unwillingly it seemed to her, his hands came up to cover hers. He rubbed his thumbs gently over her knuckles—once, twice—before disengaging her fingers. Bending low, he kissed her hands, first one then the other.

"No," he said.

She stared up at him, her face working, and for a few horrible seconds it seemed she was about to cry. Then her back stiffened. "This is not over," she said as she turned to leave. "I am not so easily set aside." He said nothing as she left the room.

Exhausted by the splendours of the evening and the crushing disappointment of its conclusion, Elizabeth slept late.

When she finally arose, she was greeted by an agitated Georgiana, who came into her room while she was still dressing and dismissed the maid. "Elizabeth," she exclaimed. "My brother will not explain why your wedding has been postponed. Please, I beg you to tell me what is going on."

Elizabeth paused in her dressing to look at her future sister. She wondered whether Mr Darcy considered his sister too young to understand or whether he was merely too embarrassed to make the explanation. Remembering his cryptic comments of the previous evening, she determined to understand the mystery of the Darcy's sojourn in Ramsgate. Carefully, she explained the nature of the accusation to Georgiana, and was heartened but not surprised by that young lady's immediate comprehension and rejection of the allegation. "It appears," she continued, "that your brother is accused of clandestine assignations in an hotel in Ramsgate last year and—" She broke off at Georgiana's cry of horror.

"Oh no, this is all my fault." She was pacing the room, shaking her head, her hands to her face, and Elizabeth was obliged to stand before her and force her to stop.

"Georgie, your brother would not explain your presence there, but you must know that you can tell me anything and be assured of my understanding and support."

Georgiana took a deep breath, nodded, and gestured to Elizabeth to join her on a small sofa. She appeared embarrassed but determined as she began her story although she could not look Elizabeth in the eye and addressed her remarks to the carpet, her voice becoming ever fainter as she told her story.

"Last year," she said, "a house was taken for me in Ramsgate, and I went there with my companion, a Mrs Younge. During my stay, we were visited by Mr Wickham, whom I knew only as a boyhood friend of my brother. He was very charming and attentive and, Elizabeth, I am very sorry to say, he persuaded me that he loved me and we ought to elope. If my brother had not arrived unexpectedly, I would have been married to that man, and my fortune would have been his."

Elizabeth patted her hands but said nothing.

"My companion was a party to Wickham's plan and was discharged. My brother also discharged my maid and the housekeeper, both of whom he had engaged and whom he thought should have informed him of my proposed trip to Scotland since they both knew of it."

Georgiana was twisting a handkerchief between her fingers. "I was greatly distressed, both by my own conduct and Mr Wickham's treachery, for I was truly convinced he loved me. Fitzwilliam was unwilling to bring me back to London in that condition, so we took rooms at an hotel since the house no longer held the staff we required." She did look up then. "Oh, Elizabeth, he was so very, very kind to me. I did not deserve his consideration, and although he was very angry, his anger was directed at Mr Wickham and his accomplice."

That, thought Elizabeth, explained so much. The depths of his animosity against Wickham, his unwillingness to discuss his presence in Ramsgate, and his avoidance of any explanation to Georgiana. Even as she reassured a distressed Georgiana, Elizabeth was trying to decide what difference the news made to her own determination to urge an early wedding.

To her disappointment, both her father and Jane agreed with Mr Darcy that a postponement was for the best; for a furious half minute, Elizabeth even suspected her sister of taking her revenge for the postponement of her own nuptials before her better nature and the memory of her sister's unfailing kindness returned. Mr Darcy was engaged throughout the morning, and she saw Colonel Fitzwilliam arrive and leave, looking furiously angry. Lord Matlock came in the afternoon and stayed for a conference with a number of gentlemen, one obviously a lawyer and one quite obviously of a much lower rank in society. Mr Handley, the secretary, was kept busy writing and receiving letters, and Elizabeth was reduced to sitting in the entrance hall, waiting for her intended to be free to meet with her.

It was not until well into the evening that she was admitted to his study. She thought he looked tired and was distressed to see him visibly summoning up the strength to resist her entreaties. "I know about Ramsgate," she said before he could speak and had the melancholy satisfaction of seeing him flinch. "I can understand why you would not wish it discussed in court, but I cannot think it at all likely. And, Fitzwilliam, I fear you are seeking reasons we should postpone our wedding rather than reasons we should not."

He closed his eyes for a moment and drew a deep breath before coming round from behind his desk. He took her hands, led her to a chair, and made her sit before kneeling at her feet. He took her hands in his, kissed them, and held them over his heart.

"Dearest," he said softly. "You must know…you cannot help but know…how very much I wish we were married. Last night in the theatre, all I could think was how it would be to be there as your husband, to have the right to hold your hand in our box or put my arm about you in our carriage. Elizabeth, I dream about you, about us, almost every night, I…"

He kissed her hands, unable to continue for a moment, and when he could, his voice was hoarse. "But no matter how much I want to be with you, I cannot. I would be coming to you tainted. Your reputation would suffer; your sisters would suffer. However much we might wish to ignore the world, the world will not ignore us, and I will not have you used for their sport."

She tried to speak, but he silenced her with a finger over her lips. "I am begging you, Elizabeth, not to make this more difficult for me. You must allow me to do what I know is right."

"And if you cannot finish this business to your satisfaction?"

"That is not an eventuality I am prepared to countenance." He got to his feet and turned away.

She, too, rose and seized his arm. "But——"

He kissed her then; he could not help it. He could not bear

to listen to her asking questions he could not answer, making demands he longed to obey. He lifted her off her feet, not noticing the weight, anxious for her silence and greedy for the touch of her mouth on his. She flung her arms about his neck, pressing against his chest, his hips, feeling him hard against her belly, and realising for the first time what it was she felt. His lips were hot against her throat, and she writhed in his arms, almost breaking his grip. She felt she was on the brink of some great discovery, something that would bind him to her utterly and forever, and she moaned as she felt the moment he regained control of himself.

He kissed her gently on the mouth and set her down on her feet. "You must go, Elizabeth," he said, and his voice was firm. "Your father is waiting for you."

As she left the room, she saw him gripping the back of his chair with both hands, his head bent, his knuckles white.

Elizabeth dreaded having to tell her mother of the postponement, knowing only too well that lady's tendency to assume the worst where her daughters' marital prospects were concerned; and indeed, Mrs Bennet's immediate reaction was exactly what her daughter might have expected.

"The wicked man!" said Mrs Bennet.

"Mama!" Elizabeth was more wearied than surprised until her mother shook her head vehemently and stamped her foot.

"I meant this Mr Holyrood, or whatever his name is. I know you think I am a great fool, Lizzy, but even I know that Mr Darcy is not the sort of gentleman who goes dangling after other men's wives. Even if he were not far too quiet and… and…respectable, a gentleman in his position can get that much more easily from a mistress."

It was lucky, reflected Elizabeth, that Mrs Gardiner and the children were not present. Her mother, of course, was all for an immediate wedding, and it is sad to reflect that it was this rather than the representations of her father and Mr Darcy that finally persuaded her that such a course was not wise. Colonel Fitzwilliam, as the one of their party most often seen in society, had undertaken to discover what was being said in the ballrooms and salons, and his news had been unpleasant.

While some people had pointed to Mr Darcy's habitual reserve and abstention from the usual fashionable vices as evidence of the falsity of the allegations, a sizeable majority were content to mock what they did not understand and mutter about 'dark horses' and 'still waters running deep' as evidence of a hidden propensity to vice. It was even said by some that his sudden marriage to a woman no one had ever heard of had been announced to throw dust in the eyes of society, for what other reason could he have for engaging himself to such an unknown?

Elizabeth had insisted on being present when this intelligence was shared and saw how deeply it affected Mr Darcy. Anger, disgust, and distress were all present in his expression, however briefly, and she was forced to recognise that her own presence added to his discomfort. Nor could she ignore the fact that her presence was preventing the gentlemen—who included not only Colonel Fitzwilliam but also Lord Matlock and Mr Laurence, the attorney—from discussing the details of the case with the frankness it required. While she privately deplored their desire to shield her from unpleasant realities, she realised that they, especially the older gentlemen, were unlikely to change for her benefit, and was obliged to withdraw.

The atmosphere in the house became ever more strained. Despite reassurances, Georgiana was convinced that she was responsible in large part for the difficulties her brother faced in fighting the case, and became anxious and withdrawn. Mr Darcy was either absent or cloistered with the gentlemen for much of the day, and when she did see him, Elizabeth could not help but recognise how weary and burdened he was. The amusements of London were closed to her sisters after an unpleasant outing to Dulwich Gallery where they were the subject of pointed silences and turned backs as soon as their identity was known.

Uneasily conscious that she was only succeeding in making those about her less happy and more uncomfortable, Elizabeth eventually agreed to leave for Scarborough with her family. Georgiana was unwilling to stay in London, and there would be no room for her and Mrs Annesley at the house Mr Bennet had taken now that Elizabeth and Jane were to travel with the rest of their family. So she returned to Pemberley, preferring the beauty of her home to the many uglinesses to be found in London.

Elizabeth came to Mr Darcy's study the night before they left; it was late, and he was still at his desk. The lamplight made the hair on his bent head shine, and she stood in the doorway for a moment, admiring his concentration on the task before him, wondering whether it was this attention to the business of life that had first attracted her. She remembered, too, how often she had been startled to see his greatcoat walking through Meryton before she remembered that he had left it with the carter's boy and it was now being worn by the boy's father. If she were honest with herself, she had never been indifferent to Darcy—intrigued, insulted, angered, and even bewildered, but never indifferent.

She said his name and saw him smile when he saw her. Mr Bennet had told him of her decision, and he was deeply grateful. As he came round his desk to her, he said as much. "I know I am asking much, dearest," he said. "But I truly believe it is for the best. You are not happy here, and what little time we can spend together is tainted."

"You will write?" He was standing before her now, and she had to look up into his face.

"Every day if you will do the same," he said. He took her hands in his and gathered them to his chest, holding them over his heart.

"Every day, I promise," she replied.

He bowed over her hands and kissed them. Not the perfunctory brush of the lips dictated by fashion, but passionately and at length as though the soft skin he found there was her lips. She shuddered, and when he released them, she raised them and touched them to her own lips. "I must not stay," she said.

"I know." He drew in a breath. "Never doubt that I wish you could stay, but you must go."

She raised herself on her toes, he bent his head, and they kissed briefly before she turned on her heel and fled. The next day as she left in the carriage with her father and Jane, her last sight of him was of him standing on the stairs of Darcy House, his hands clasped behind his back, the rigidity of his stance a testament to the unhappiness he would not, and perhaps could not, express in any other way.

CHAPTER 27

LETTERS

EXTRACTS FROM THE CORRESPONDENCE OF MR FITZWILLIAM Darcy and Miss Elizabeth Bennet.

Darcy House, Grosvenor Square
London

Dearest,
Although I know you will not arrive in Scarborough for another two days, I have taken the liberty of writing to you now, partly I must acknowledge because I miss talking with you, and this is a method, no matter how imperfect, whereby I may share my thoughts with you.

I have spent so many years as sole arbiter of my own fate—and indeed, of the fate of those about me—that it is a strange, almost luxurious, sensation to have another person in whom I may confide, safe in the knowledge that I shall be understood and that our interests and hopes are closely aligned. I do not expect that we shall always agree. We are neither of us as complacent (and I am certainly not as agreeable) as Bingley and Miss Bennet, but we are in sympathy, are we not, my love?

There is no news since you left save that Colonel Fitzwilliam has received orders to embark his regiment for Spain. He will be greatly missed and not only for his assistance in our trouble. The intention is for the regiment to spend time in Portugal, finishing its training, before the campaigning season next year. His easy manners and fashionable habits make it easy to forget that he is a seasoned and valuable soldier who is, I know, much caressed by his superiors. I have known him all my life and fear for his safety although I do not, of course, express this to my sister, who leaves for Pemberley tomorrow. Do I ask too much if I request you to write to her as well as to me? I know she is coming to feel considerable affection for you, and I am anxious that we both do our best to ensure she does not feel lonely or neglected. She has spent too much time alone, a mistake of mine I intend to do my best to rectify in the coming months.

I must go. Mr Laurence has arrived, and I must meet with him. I await with impatience your first letter although I know it will be several days before it can arrive. May I ask you to tell me of your days, where you go, and who you see? I am, I confess, greedy for your news.

Ever your most humble and devoted servant,
Fitzwilliam Darcy

The George Hotel, Stamford

My Dear Fitzwilliam,
This is the first time I have written your name, and I confess to some satisfaction in so doing. I know I cannot expect a letter from you until I arrive in Scarborough, but we are stopped for the night, and I cannot sleep.

The carriage is most comfortable and your people attentive and considerate, but I must admit I am already weary of the journey. Father has his nose in a book, and Jane is forever commenting upon the absence of Mr Bingley in a manner so patient and uncomplaining that I am already driven to contemplate screaming. Worst of all is the knowledge that I am being taken ever further from you.

I am relying upon you not to hide things from me. Whatever the truth, no matter how painful or indelicate you might consider it to be, please do not conceal it from me. My exile in the North will, I have no doubt, be comfortable, but it will still be an exile. I beg you not to deny me the exile's comfort of news from home.

I know that a young lady is not supposed to reveal her affections in her correspondence, but it is well that you realise at an early date what an improper bride you have chosen for yourself since I have no hesitation in declaring that I already miss you greatly and long for the time when we can be together again.

Your impenitent
Elizabeth

Darcy House, Grosvenor Square
London

My Dear Elizabeth,

Your letter was an unexpected joy at the beginning of a busy and disheartening day. Thank you.

In reply to your request for news: Laurence has hired a Bow Street Runner to search for the suborned witnesses, servants from the White Horse at Ramsgate. However, he has had but little success so far, and it seems likely that they have been sequestered somewhere.

Our enquiries about Hollernshaw have been more successful. He is an MP and sits for a pocket borough near Lancaster, and it appears that it is only his seat in Parliament that is protecting him from arrest for debt. Although we have discovered that his debts have arisen from unwise speculation, we have been unable to discover its precise nature or the amount of his indebtedness.

My friend Meopham accused him of avarice, and my own opinion of the man, formed during our only meeting earlier this year, was also of a man more concerned with matters financial than with family loyalty, let alone affection. It has been my expe-rience that such men, while anxious to hold on to what is theirs, can often be tempted into rash action by the lure of unusually large gains, and it is, of course, such gambles that most often leave their investors out of pocket.

However, be that as it may, the owner of the pocket borough is a friend of my uncle Matlock and is prepared to sell the borough to me in return for my uncle's support in the Lords and assurance that my nominee will further the same interests. With an election expected in the autumn, I can ensure that Hollernshaw loses both his seat and his protection from the sponging house. I cannot and do not approve of the way seats in Parliament are currently bestowed, but until such time as reform is made, I feel justified in making use of the anomaly.

There, that is all the news I have to impart.

I fear I am no more a proper gentleman than you are a young lady since I, too, have no hesitation in saying how very much I miss you. For the first time ever, the house seems overly quiet to me. Hitherto, I have always tried to be content with my life and my work, and I am now obliged to acknowledge that neither is sufficient.

Your humble and devoted servant,
Fitzwilliam

Promenade House, South Shore
Scarborough

My Dearest,
Firstly, this is a delightful house, high on the cliffs and with a beautiful prospect. Thank you for arranging it. I have never before seen the sea, and I confess it is not at all as I imagined it. Despite all the descriptions in books and despite all the paintings and pictures, I had somehow assumed it to be blue, not the grey-green colour I can see from my window. Nor had I realised quite how relentless the movement and sound are. As I re-read this, I realise just how foolish this seems but I believe I had better display all my folly at the beginning of our correspondence so that you may become inured to it before we are married.

Mr Bingley arrived yesterday and is staying with his sister who, you may remember, withdrew here some weeks ago. He and Jane have announced that they are not prepared to wait any longer for their marriage, and since Mr Bingley has come furnished with a special licence, the wedding has been set for Saturday next. Although I shall miss Jane greatly, I can see the justice of their decision and have done my best to suppress my own jealousy and participate fully in the preparations.

Jane and Miss Bingley met at the house Mr Bingley has taken for his sister, and Jane tells me that 'dear Caroline' has been kindness itself. I am endeavouring to hide my suspicions about that lady's true feelings since Jane will not believe me and would only be distressed if I succeeded in convincing her. However, I am natural philosopher enough to anticipate my own first meeting with Miss Bingley with considerable interest.

Thank you so very much for all your news. I know it cannot be easy to write of these things, and I am more grateful than you can know. Not to know would be bitter indeed and serve only to increase my sense of isolation despite the all-too-obvious presence of my family, much though I love them.

With regard to the nature of That Man's speculation, have you considered consulting my uncle Gardiner who has many friends and acquaintances on 'Change? And I have been wondering why you do not simply reveal Lord Meopham's wishes for his sister's legacy.

See what a managing wife you shall have.

Your impatient betrothed,
Elizabeth

Darcy House, Grosvenor Square
London

Dearest Elizabeth,
I received a letter from my sister today and must thank you for taking the time to write to her. I also received a letter from Bingley, which I assume is an announcement of his nuptials, since I have utterly failed to decipher more than the occasional line. I devoutly trust your sister will take on the burden of family correspondence in the future.

I took your excellent advice about consulting Mr Gardiner, and he has already introduced me to several gentlemen who have provided useful information. It seems the speculation was of the most foolish kind and Hollernshaw's losses were heavy indeed. I have purchased a proportion of his debts sufficient to ruin him. If the election takes place before the courts begin sitting at Michaelmas, I can force him into either debtor's prison or into leaving the country. However, I am reluctant to do so before he is obliged to withdraw the accusation since that would leave the allegation before the world uncontested. It would be all too easy for the world to say that I have used my wealth and position to kill an action I would otherwise have lost. I admit that, at the moment, I can see no way around this dilemma.

You ask about my friend's will. Unfortunately, his wishes were expressed to me personally and are not included in the body of his will. This is perfectly legal; I understand from Laurence that it is known as a 'secret trust'. Poor Meopham was concerned that, if the legacy was known to Hollernshaw, he would make demands upon me or, still worse, upon his sister. How correct he has proven to be, we all now know.

As for me, I am well. London is uncomfortable and hot, but at least this has driven most of society and its curiosity away. I am considering having a shower bath installed here, just for this time of year. I do not know whether you have ever seen one. One stands under a pipe with a rose, like a watering can, and water is poured from above. It can be most refreshing, and now I come to think of it, there is no reason why the water should not be warm in winter. I shall ask Mrs Tate to make enquiries.

I have written to Bingley with my regrets that I shall not be able to attend the wedding; with so much to do and so little time in which to do it, I do not feel I can leave London. Please assure your sister of my best and kindest wishes and of my confidence in her future happiness.

I must confess that I, too, need on occasion to suppress feelings of some little jealousy of Bingley and your sister. If it were not for the person you refer to as That Man, we would now be enjoying married life at Pemberley. The fact that such enjoyment is denied us is not the smallest of the debts I charge to him and for which I shall demand a reckoning.

I wish you were here, dearest. I wish I had thought to have some little painting, or even a silhouette made, so that I might have something of you to look at. I fear I am become as foolish a lover as any in literature.

Your humble and devoted servant,
Fitzwilliam

Promenade House, South Shore
Scarborough.

My Dear, Dear, very Dear Fitzwilliam,
If I did not already suspect you to be the most generous of men, the arrival of my aunt Gardiner and the children would have confirmed it. I know my aunt has already written to express her appreciation of your care and that of your people, but I thought you might like to know that, according to her, if Young Tom ever decides to abandon his ambitions to be a coachman, he may be assured of her recommendation as a nursery maid and that, thanks to his father, Robert, Matthew. and Amelia are all resolved to be coachmen when they grow up.

The presence of the children has been a particular joy to Kitty and me. Mama and Jane are entangled in preparations for the wedding, and my aunt is helping to keep my mother within the bounds of taste and reasonable economy. Papa is trying to extend his influence over his younger daughters, starting with Mary who, he says, has at least the habit of concentration, even if that concentration is usually ill-applied. He is trying to extend her interests beyond the sermons and books of conduct that have hitherto formed the majority of her reading. He began with that book you gave her about the Psalms and is currently introducing her to the poems of Herbert.

Lydia was much fatigued by the journey and spends most of the day in bed. This has left Kitty and me somewhat at a loss for occupation, especially Kitty since I at least have my daily correspondence to attend to. Expeditions with children to the beach and to the harbour have been a welcome addition to our day. On the one day we were rained indoors, I remembered you saying that you had no picture of me, so I have enclosed four. I particularly admire Amelia's attention to my hair although, in case you have forgotten, may I assure you that I do not have six fingers on one hand and four on the other. Kitty's effort is perhaps a little ambitious, but the head and shoulders are not unlike, so perhaps it will do until something better can be obtained.

Well, my dear sir, you did say you wished to hear of my day. I am trying to possess my soul in patience, but I cannot walk as I do at home and find myself becoming increasingly restless. And yet I do not sleep! I wake ever earlier and must lie there for fear of waking the house, and I cannot prevent my mind retracing the past and seeking to trace the future. This morning, I must have lain there for over an hour wondering what would become of Mrs Hollernshaw. If her husband wins, she might easily be set aside by a man so devoid of decency and will not even have the comfort of her legacy. If he loses, I cannot believe he will suddenly decide to treat her well, and yet she will be obliged to follow him into disgrace.

I am sorry this letter sounds so despondent. I shall endeavour to be more active tomorrow in the hope that I might sleep better at night. I shall also do my best to be more my usual self in my next letter. In any event, I believe we both know what I require to effect a permanent improvement in my disposition, and it remains in London for the foreseeable future.

Your mumpish betrothed,
Elizabeth

Darcy House, Grosvenor Square
London

My Dearest,
Your letter has become the most eagerly anticipated event of my day. The weather is oppressively hot, our business has progressed no further than it had in my last, and I miss your presence greatly.

I went into the mistress's apartments last night just to remember you sitting there. The furniture seems to me acceptable, although you must feel free to change anything you wish, but the wallpaper is sadly faded. I enclose a number of sample sheets. If nothing suits your fancy, you must say so, or if one or other is almost what you would wish, you have but to say, and I shall send more samples. However, if one is acceptable, I can arrange for the paper-hanging to take place while you are away. I want you to make this house your own.

Thank you for the pictures, and please extend my thanks to the artists. Miss Catherine does indeed show some promise as an artist. Perhaps your father should consider hiring a master. There are several such in Scarborough during the season. I have happy memories of the place, and indeed, I stayed with my nurse in the very house currently occupied by Mrs Gardiner. I was sent there as a child several times when my cough was particularly troublesome because the sea air was the only effective palliative. I believe Nanny Grayson still retains my little wooden spade. I remember spending hours on the sand, digging holes, making sandcastles, never caring that the tide always came and erased them, and eager to return the next day and start all over again. I do not think I was ever as happy as a child—alone but not lonely, engrossed, content merely to be able to breathe without difficulty as I laboured. When it rained, there was a window seat in my bedroom where I could sit to read and watch the waves. I have been fond of window seats ever since and strongly believe that every child's room should contain one.

I am ashamed to say I had given little consideration to Mrs Hollernshaw's plight beyond my determination to preserve her legacy and promise I shall attempt to think of some way to preserve her respectability and peace of mind. I cannot, however, promise I shall be successful as this business seems to become ever more complicated as we proceed.

I have racked my brains for some way in which I might come to Scarborough for Bingley's wedding to your sister, and there is none. The journey there and back could not take much less than a week, and however much I wish I could see you, I cannot risk leaving London for an extended period when our affairs are in such a state of confusion. This realisation has soured my disposition so thoroughly that I fear for That Man's health and continued existence should I meet him in the street.

I am sorry you are feeling so low and recognise only too well the sensation of exhausted wakefulness you describe. Might I suggest that you do not attempt to tire yourself with additional activity as this will only add to your fatigue without helping you to sleep. In my experience, only a calm mind and hope for the future will do that, although I realise how difficult it is to conjure either at will.

Try to remember how very much you are loved and how very much I anticipate seeing you once more as soon as this wretched business is settled.

I kiss your hands, especially the six-fingered one.

Ever your humble and devoted servant,
Fitzwilliam

Promenade House, South Shore
Scarborough

My dear Fitzwilliam,
It is too bad of me to add to your difficulties by burdening you with my trivial ones. In truth, there is nothing wrong with me,

save for boredom and missing you, and both will be cured as soon as we meet again. The wedding takes place the day after tomorrow. Jane will look beautiful, and your humble servant will do her best not to disgrace the scene.

I conveyed your suggestion about a master for Kitty to my father, and once I assured him the master in question was a dyspeptic, German gentleman of grandfatherly appearance, he was retained. Kitty's skill is already showing considerable improvement, as I believe you can see from the enclosed. As for the wallpaper, the one you numbered 3 is my favourite. Unless you can find one where the pink is less prominent, I believe it will do very well for the bedroom.

Poor Lydia, on the other hand, is showing little sign of improvement. Although she has left her bed, she refuses to leave the house unless my father accompanies her because she is so very afraid. There are militia quartered in the castle, and at the first sight of a soldier, she became completely hysterical. My father is talking of moving the family after the wedding, and much as I shall regret leaving here, I believe he may be correct. Although no one hopes for the return of her former heedless confidence, this abject terror is pitiable to behold.

We had dinner with the Bingleys and Hursts last night, and I must confess that Miss Bingley was all friendliness and complacence, at least so far as my dear Jane was concerned. I do not recall that she exchanged more than the merest civilities with me. However, since even so little politesse is an improvement on our earlier intercourse, I have decided to return like for like while always remembering to keep my powder dry in case it is required later.

And now the seamstress has arrived. It appears that I have lost weight since this gown was originally made, and I must have it adjusted if I am to do credit to the family.

And with that demonstration of vanity, I must sign myself
Your loving,
Elizabeth

Promenade House, South Shore
Scarborough
11.30pm

Dearest Fitzwilliam,
I wish I could claim that two letters in one day is evidence of
absence performing its usual transformation upon my heart;
however, I am so very, very angry, I am instead taking a few
minutes to dash this down on paper although I am unsure as yet
whether or not I shall post it.

I withdraw everything even remotely complimentary that I have
ever said about Miss Caroline Bingley. Both families gathered for
a last dinner before the wedding, and she had the unmitigated gall
to insinuate (after the ladies had retired, of course) that according
to the gossip of the town, Mrs Hollernshaw had been seen entering
Darcy House with her child. She insinuated that, in those circles
of society in which I shall be moving, I must expect my husband to
have his 'amusements' and that, if I am not prepared to accept
this, I should step aside for someone who will (and I think we can
all surmise who was meant). I, of course, replied that I thought
better of your morals, your manners, and your intelligence than to
suppose that you would entertain your mistress in the house we
were soon to share. I also pointed out that Mrs Hollernshaw is a
most unhappy lady who needs all the friends who are prepared to
stand by her, amongst whom I hoped one day to be numbered. I
then turned the conversation very determinedly to wallpaper and
had the satisfaction of drawing my mother into an interminable
discussion of the advantages of stripes over flowers, during which I
am for once glad to say Miss Bingley did not manage to contribute
another word.

I am relieved that Jane was not a party to this exchange, and is even now endeavouring to sleep in the room next to mine. Judging by the sound of footsteps, she is having as little success as I am, so I had better go in and attempt to calm her enough to retire for the night.

Merely writing down the source of my annoyance has acted as a most effective cure, so I believe I shall get sleep enough to avoid the dark circles under my eyes my mother has been predicting with enthusiasm for the last several days.

Your stalwart if irritated,
Elizabeth

Promenade House, South Shore
Scarborough

Dearest
If you have not already read my last, please do not. I was in an angry mood when I wrote it and had no intention of posting it; however, Sarah, in a sudden fit of efficiency, had it sent to the post office while I was bathing. I cannot write more now, we leave for the church very shortly, but I would infinitely prefer it if you did not read that letter.

Yours in haste,
Elizabeth

Darcy House, Grosvenor Square
London

My dearest love,
I leave for Scarborough within the hour; only the fact that I must

travel by coach for much of the way will ensure this letter arrives before I do. The case is abandoned, Hollernshaw is beaten hands down, and is fleeing the country. Mrs Hollernshaw arrived here several days ago with her husband's papers, which reveal so flagrant and despicable a conspiracy to defraud that even his seat in Parliament will not serve to protect him.

I dared not write sooner for fear of exciting expectations that might not be met; however, I can now state triumphantly that no work of man can prevent or delay our wedding.

Your trousseau travels with me—would you care to be married from Pemberley, my darling?

Yours in haste and triumph,
Fitzwilliam

CHAPTER 28

LOVER'S MEETING

Trip no further, pretty sweeting
Journey's end in Lovers' meeting
Every wise man's son doth know.
—Shakespeare, Twelfth Night

THE DAY AFTER JANE'S WEDDING, THE WEATHER BROKE. IN place of the brilliant sunshine that had graced the ceremony, the skies were overcast, and a thin, penetrating drizzle fell, depressing the spirits and driving everyone indoors. Mrs Bennet complained every few minutes of the dullness and the loss of her dear Jane. Elizabeth, who perhaps of all the family most truly missed her sister, was driven to her room and her correspondence to escape.

On the Tuesday, there was no letter from Mr Darcy and although two arrived the following day, somehow that did not make up for the missing daily delivery. On Thursday, the letter announcing his arrival and the successful end to the suit was delivered, and Mrs Bennet was once more cast into transports of expectation and preparation. Elizabeth knew there was no point in writing to him again while he was on the road, and was reduced to calculating and recalculating how quickly he could arrive. The newspapers seemed full of news of carriage accidents and highway robberies, and she had almost succeeded in fretting herself into a decline when, on the Friday afternoon, the weather cleared and Mr Bennet strongly advised her to borrow Young Tom from Mrs Gardiner and take herself off for a long walk. As she left the house on the cliffs, she could hear her mother wailing her protests behind her.

She could hear the soldiers in the castle were at musket practice, so she headed inland towards the woods above Scarborough and the York Road. It was, she told herself severely, far too early to expect Mr Darcy, but it could do no harm, surely, to look. The ground was just soft enough underfoot to make the walk pleasant without being too muddy, and although Young Tom carried an umbrella, she thought the chances of her having to make use of it were small.

As she strode up the hill away from the town, she could feel her spirits start to lift. This was what she had needed, and she blessed her father's thought of Young Tom as an escort. He at least was active enough to keep up with her, unlike the maids, poor things, who were wont to complain after a mile or two. The leaves were just starting to change; she had always loved the colours of autumn and fell to imagining the woods about Pemberley, utterly fettered by her complete lack of any accurate information on the subject.

They reached the top of the hill, and she looked back at the sea, once again sparkling in the sun as it rose and fell against the sandy beach where she had played with her young cousins. She decided that they would bring their children here one day and see the little piles of sandy boots and shoes in the hallways, the tiny wooden spades and buckets. She would love to watch a storm at sea at least once in her life. She flung out her arms and drew in a breath of salty air; life seemed once more full of possibilities, and she was conscious of her enormous good fortune. He was coming, and her life would never be the same again, and she was so very, very thankful.

She turned her back on the town and struck out through the woods and towards the main road. She could see for miles from this vantage point, and it seemed but one more gift amongst all those with which she had been blessed that, in the distance, she could see *him* astride a great, grey horse, galloping towards her.

She ran down, hearing the heavy boots of Young Tom behind her, until she reached the road, stopping to catch her breath as she waited for him to come up to her. He had seen her and urged his horse to even greater efforts until he drew to a halt before her, scattering the gravel, dismounting almost before the horse had stopped.

They were on the public highway, and Young Tom was standing stolidly a little way off, so they could not embrace as she knew they both wished, but they could look. He bowed over her hand. "Miss Bennet."

"Mr Darcy." She curtseyed, suddenly shy.

"Shall we?" She took the proffered arm, and Young Tom leading the horse at a discreet distance, all three headed back towards the town. There was so much news to share that they scarcely knew where to begin and eventually settled on the fate of That Man and the court case.

"Once again, dearest Elizabeth," he said. "I am indebted to you for your advice. I arranged for Laurence's Bow Street Runner to meet up with Mrs Hollernshaw while she was at Sunday Service to assure her that, whatever the outcome of the case, I held myself bound to provide both the value of her brother's legacy and whatever assistance she required to live apart from her husband. The next day she arrived on my doorstep with her daughter and the contents of her husband's desk. They include correspondence with the suborned witnesses, including their complaints that he was not paying them enough to perjure themselves. We swore out criminal information against him with the magistrates, but he got wind of what we were about and fled." He laughed grimly. "He was trying to get to America from Liverpool but had insufficient funds and is currently, I understand, stranded on the Isle of Man, where he can afford only the meanest of accommodation."

"And Mrs Hollernshaw?"

"Is understandably distressed by the whole business. She has gone to Harrogate to take the waters for a while before deciding whether to live at her brother's cottage or sell it and live elsewhere. She is worried that she might be ostracised following the scandal, although I believe I can muster enough credit in the neighbourhood to ensure that she is treated with respect. If you and I and our friends visit, there are few who will dare stay away." He heard her giggle at this and looked down. "Oh dear, did that sound very pompous?"

"Perhaps a little, but it is in a good cause, so I believe I shall overlook it on this occasion." Unseen by Young Tom, he brought her hand to his lips, and they walked in contented silence for a little way before he thought to enquire after the recent wedding.

"It was quite the most beautiful wedding I have ever seen—"

"To date!"

"To date," she agreed happily. "Jane was so very happy and Mr Bingley so very dazed that, even had they both been ill-favoured, I believe everyone would have agreed. I do not think either of them heard a word anyone said between the church and their leaving for their honeymoon. My cousin Amelia was rather struck and has been playing at weddings with her dolls ever since." She looked down and bit her lip. "You will be pleased to know that I bridesmaided with great aplomb, I do not think anyone realised just how jealous I was." She looked up into his face and blushed at his expression.

"We leave tomorrow, my darling, if I have to pack everyone's luggage myself." He pulled off his riding gloves and stuck them in his pocket so that they could hold hands, skin to skin. "I have written to Pemberley and to the church at Lambton. I am afraid you will have to reconcile yourself to a church full of people you have never seen before since half the town appears bent on attending. Then I shall drag you away from your family for our honeymoon. I thought you might like to visit the Lake District."

They were passing through a small copse of trees, and with a nod to Young Tom, he seized her by the hand and pulled her behind a thick clump of young oaks. There was a pile of fallen timber, and he lifted her up to stand upon it. She was laughing until he kissed her. She had re-lived his kisses a hundred times, but she had still forgotten; she had forgotten the strength of his arms and the warm, firm tenderness of his lips. She seized his lapels to draw him closer and then had to hang on to them for support when his tongue brushed against hers. Her heart was hammering in her chest, and she was conscious of the press of her breasts against his waistcoat and the faint brush of the cloth that covered them. All at once, suddenly and shockingly, she longed to lie with him. She knew only what her aunt Gardiner had told her, for she utterly discounted her mother's vague murmurings, but she had gathered that, with a gentle and loving husband, it could be glorious. If it was as good as this, then with the addition of privacy and the right to touch and hold, it must be truly wonderful.

But not here. She felt the exact moment they both realised they must stop. He lifted his head, and she rested hers on his chest while they both fought for control. Then, after a few minutes, he helped her down from her perch, retrieved his hat from where he had dropped it, and they walked back to the road.

As they entered the town, they saw Caroline Bingley in the distance, just coming out of a shop on Huntriss Row. Elizabeth saw him frown and realised he had received her unfortunate letter. She was about to say something when he spoke. "I really must commend Miss Bingley on the speed of her communications with London," he said. "Let us see how long it takes news to travel in the opposite direction." And Elizabeth realised he intended to cut her dead.

Although she held no brief for Miss Bingley, this seemed altogether too cruel to her, so she curtseyed in that lady's general direction and had the satisfaction of seeing an expression of utmost mortification on that discontented face while she herself had been nothing but kind—a distinction she had difficulty in explaining to her betrothed, who was disinclined to mercy where anyone who offended his future wife was concerned. It was a discussion that, although they did not realise it, was to reoccur many times in their marriage without ever reaching a satisfactory resolution.

They strolled together towards the house in the late afternoon sunshine, their shadows stretching out before them as their new lives unfurled. A marriage that was to last fifty-three years with some sorrows but many more joys, a life full of active benevolence, happiness, and laughter. A marriage that extended to welcome in Anne De Bourgh when her mother died, and gave her a life so much happier and healthier than any she had known hitherto. A marriage that brought them two children: a daughter with her mother's liveliness and her father's musicianship, who on her marriage became one of Victorian England's greatest supporters and patrons of the arts; and a son who combined his father's industry and his mother's compassion to become both entrepreneur and philanthropist. Darcyville, the model village he built for his work people, still stands today, a monument to a family for whom love was not merely a word but the backbone and breath of everything they thought and did.

THE END

The favor of your review is always appreciated.

Subscribers to the Quills & Quartos mailing list receive bonus content, advance notice of sales, and alerts for new releases. You can join the mailing list at www.QuillsandQuartos.com

ACKNOWLEDGMENTS

The Author would like to thank Marcelle Gibson for her unfailing encouragement and her Mum for her hospitality. I would say during the pandemic but I, like the rest of her children, grandchildren and great-grandchildren, know we're always welcome

ABOUT THE AUTHOR

Catherine Lodge is a retired English lawyer and lecturer, currently living in North Yorkshire. She spends her days reading, admits to a slightly shame-faced addiction to Minecraft, and volunteers to explain IT to the senior citizens at her local library (despite the fact that some of them are younger than she is). She is also prepared to send a fifty-pound/dollar/euro Amazon gift card to the first person who can prove that Colonel Fitzwilliam's first name is Richard. So there.

You can reach her at catherinelodgebooks@gmail.com, and she would love to hear from you.

Fair Stands the Wind

We all know that, in Jane Austen's *Pride & Prejudice*, Mr. Darcy is proud and prejudiced because he is a wealthy landowner who believes himself above his company and that Elizabeth Bennet can afford to be proud and prejudiced because she believes she has the freedom to make choices for herself.

But what if Mr. Darcy is the second son, sent to sea at a young age? What if Elizabeth is trapped by circumstances with an ill father on one side and an understandably desperate mother on the other?

Meet Captain Darcy of the Royal Navy, a successful frigate captain with ample prize money and a sister for whom he needs to provide while he is at sea. Meet also Elizabeth Bennet, who needs a husband and is trying to resign herself to Mr. Collins, the worst 'least worst alternative' in the history of literature.

Made in the USA
Monee, IL
22 October 2022

16393141R00125